Lithium & Let's Plays

Kelly Waters

Cover design by Bia S.
Edited by Mallory Day

Revised Edition
ISBN (paperback): 979-8-9993113-0-6
ISBN (eBook): 979-8-9993113-1-3
ISBN (Hardcover): 979-8-9993113-2-0
Printed in the United States of America

For more information, visit: https://kellychyllenewrites.com/

Trigger Warnings

This book explores mental health experiences, including bipolar disorder, manic psychosis, and the impacts of addiction and substance use. It contains depictions of hospitalization, therapy, and recovery that may be triggering for some readers.

Please take care of yourself and be mindful of your well-being before reading.

For my friends and family who have had my back through my mental health journey, and for anyone like me who wanted to see themselves in a character when they felt alone.

Table of Contents

Chapter One
The Chase

Tess ran through an open field. Pounding footsteps sounded behind her, and she pushed the run to a sprint. The little stamina she had left quickly depleted, but stopping wasn't an option. It had been a while since she'd seen any resources to replenish her energy, and the stalker was closing in on her.

"Just a little further until the next town," she reminded herself, but the steps echoed even closer. The next town wouldn't be close enough.

Tess waved her hand, and a steep wooden ramp materialized in the empty field before her. If she couldn't outrun the stalker, she would at least get a height advantage on them.

She sprinted up the ramp, reaching the top in moments, then spun around and motioned her hands again. A floor formed beneath her feet as four wooden walls materialized around it, effectively enclosing her body inside a wide box. The walls blocked her view of the field, so she jumped and formed a small ramp beneath her feet.

At the sight of her building, the stalker had begun his own.

His sunflower sunglasses bobbed on his face as he formed a ramp far from her base, but he continued to build in an upward diagonal, slowly approaching her. She was, of course, expecting this and already had an assault rifle lined up to his position.

One shot brought down half his health, the next missed, and the last finished him off. The items he had collected spilled out from his body as he disappeared into nothing.

Tess felt the tension in her shoulders dissipate with a satisfying exhale and couldn't help laughing at the heap of golden items that spilled over his base. He hadn't put up much of a fight for the inventory he was working with.

That's when she heard a new shot, and before she had time to surround herself with more cover, the entire world around her faded.

Game Over

"God DAMNIT! I WAS PEEKING OUT LIKE A TOTAL BOT!" Tess screamed. She released an angry breath, scanning the messy living room she had made home for her gaming setup. "I can't play many more solos like this."

She blinked at the homepage of her video game, DuskCabins, an online, multiplayer, free battle royale sweeping the gaming industry. To win, you just had to be the last player alive.

Tess had always loved playing video games, and right now, she had more time to dedicate to mastering DuskCabins than any game she'd played before. At the same time, her skills were not up to par with what they used to be; her energy, her reaction time, even her thinking was stilted as she continued to recover from mania.

Still, playing this game seemed to be the only thing that pulled her away from the reality of her current situation, or worse, the memory of all that she'd just been through.

She closed her laptop with a sigh. It was a graduation gift from her dad. He'd found it online for a good deal, and it was intended for her college studies. It certainly wasn't designed to run graphically complicated programs, but on very low graphics settings, Tess had DuskCabins working successfully.

She unplugged her external mouse, headset, and keyboard, then carried the laptop out of the room.

She had dropped out of college for the semester, and now her days were spent sleeping, attending group therapy, and playing

DuskCabins. It was a hard decision to make, but she had missed too many classes during her three-week hospital stay to catch up. Now, she was meant to focus on recovery full-time.

From one glance around the kitchen, she knew what everyone had eaten for breakfast. Her dad's used pan of eggs was sitting on the stove, her mother's cereal box at the table, and her brother's half-eaten toast still littered his plate at the counter.

She sighed and started moving the dishes to the sink. It was already overflowing with pots and pans, but she carefully balanced them on top.

She missed the small college apartment that had begun to feel like a new home to her, where she had complete control over the atmosphere.

Her mother kept reminding her that she would be back there soon, but until then, the world felt like it moved in slow motion. From where she stood, it was hard to see the other side of the mountain.

Sometimes, she didn't feel positive she'd ever see the other side again.

Tess prayed silently that someone had gone grocery shopping, but inside the fridge, just five take-out containers lined the shelves. There was one drawer with a few deli meats, but she could tell they were long expired from the smell.

She reheated what was left in a Chinese takeout container and settled down at the kitchen table, opening her laptop once more. Her laptop screen glowed purple as she brought up her current favorite source of entertainment, Twitch. When Tess wasn't playing DuskCabins, she liked to watch people stream the video game online. By watching the bigger streamers, she absorbed the latest strategies.

The game was continuously updated, so it was hard to keep up otherwise. She'd learn what in-game items to prioritize, given the limited inventory space, and new tips for build fighting. Build fighting was precisely what had just happened in Tess's last game, when players were not only trying to shoot each other, but also crafting defensive structures simultaneously.

She clicked on her favorite streamer's channel. He played for one of the most popular Esports teams, EFN Perktuns. He had a live video streaming titled "Let's Play DuskCabins!". He was competing in a duo with a player she hadn't heard of before, Sizzars.

She moved her cursor to the search bar and typed in Sizzars's name. Sure enough, he was another streamer, but only with a few thousand followers. Comparatively, Perktuns had three million.

She always liked to watch smaller streamers like Sizzars. Their chats moved slower, their skill levels were more achievable, and they tended to interact more personally with their viewers. She avoided talking in chats herself but liked to observe the conversations that took place.

Sizzars and Perktuns played on a team of two until Perktuns ended his stream and left the party. With the departure of his duo, Sizzars's stream numbers dropped from a couple thousand to a couple hundred, the chat slowed down drastically.

"Thanks to all the new viewers for checking out my stream! Perktuns is a dope streamer, so if anyone from my community hasn't checked out his gameplay before, be sure to drop him a follow and say that I sent you."

Tess laughed at the unlikely idea that any of these people had played DuskCabins and hadn't heard of Perktuns. He was practically at the top of everyone's home screen when they opened Twitch.

She watched Sizzars play a few more games, but without Perktuns's help, he had really lost his mojo. As she studied his tactics for fighting three players at once, her fork scratched against a now empty take-out container. She walked across the kitchen and threw it away.

With a glance at the clock, she tensed, anticipating her brother Daniel's arrival. His bus would drop him back off from school any moment. Simultaneously, she became aware of the heaviness of her eyelids as her afternoon exhaustion began to sink in. She grabbed her laptop and went upstairs.

The buzz of Sizzars's stream still filled her bedroom as she stripped off her day clothes in exchange for an oversized t-shirt. By now, Sizzars was playing with a different friend with the gamertag, BlackLantern.

After a few moments, she observed BlackLantern as a much better player than Sizzars. She wondered why big Esports players even bothered with Sizzars, although where his skill lacked, his personality seemed to take over. She laughed as he convinced BlackLantern to get on a military truck and then sent him flying off the side of the map. He died instantly.

She hadn't remembered any mention of BlackLantern in the Esports scene before. After a quick search on Twitch with no results, her eyebrows rose. She had thought every half-decent DuskCabins player wanted to be a streamer. It was possible he was too young to stream.

"I got an extra shotty if you want it, Siz?" Lantern grunted.

She hadn't given his voice distinct attention up to this point, but now she could tell it certainly did not belong to a younger kid. She glanced at the chat, which had slowed down to thirty viewers, and her curiosity took over. She decided to inquire about him there.

> **JustaTesst: Where's this Lantern Guy's stream?**
> **TylerGames: He doesn't have one! We keep telling him to stream!!**
> **Raaaacheal: Yeah, who doesn't want to listen to that voice more?**

She rolled her eyes. Sometimes the way other gamers talked in Twitch chats made her feel nauseous. She couldn't count how many people out there perpetuated the sweaty live-in-their-mom's-basement stereotype. She frowned as she remembered, in her current situation, she might as well fall into that category.

"OH, hello, Just-a?! Welcome to my stream! Yeah, that's my buddy Lantern back from my COD days. He's a beast but not much of an entertainer. Are you enjoying the stream so far?"

"Shit," she muttered. She'd been spotted by Sizzars. She generally avoided the chat feature because of these cringy, forced conversations. Smaller streamers were always desperate to rope more people into their community.

She rolled her eyes, partially at herself, and typed out a response. From what she'd observed, she could learn a lot from BlackLantern if he were a streamer.

JustaTesst: Yeah, it's cool! Keep it up. #GetLanternaStream2020

Her face turned red at the poor attempt at humor, but she reasoned with herself: What did she have to lose? It was just the internet. She would likely never interact with any of these people again. Before any other users in the chat—or worse—Sizzars, could respond, she pushed the top of her laptop down.

Next to her bed, a plastic pill case labeled with the days of the week rested on a small table. There was a glass of water beside it that her mother refilled every day, whether the cup was empty or not.

She opened the plastic square marked "Tuesday" and pulled out a small arrangement of white and salmon-colored pills. Sleep came easily—it always had since the mania faded—and it was always dark and dreamless.

Chapter Two
Doing the Time

A warm beam of sunlight danced across Tess's room, pulling her from her slumber. She glanced toward the light source and met her mother's gaze. She softly smiled at Tess as she pushed open the rest of the curtains.

Tess groaned and rubbed her eyes. "Wh-what time is it?"

"Good morning," her mother said softly. "It's only nine, but your group is at ten. I think it's important that you're eating meals at the right time." She frowned and looked out the window. "Are you okay to drive?"

"I don't know..."

She'd driven a few times since she returned home, but with all the medications, she was feeling anxious about it. Her psychiatrist assured the family that she was fine to drive, but she still didn't feel like her old self.

It wasn't necessarily her cognitive ability as much as it was her depleted confidence after the breakdown. At first, her mother drove her over to her group, but now she started work again.

"Well, I have to get to work at nine-thirty...but you could take an Uber...it would just be expensive, and your dad, well, you know, he thinks you should..." Her voice trailed off.

Tess wondered what she was going to say. Should be driving more? Should be working? Should be back at school? Should be less sick? Tess agreed.

"I'll drive," Tess said flatly as she rolled out of bed and walked to her dresser. "Now, can I get some privacy?"

"Okay...but Tess?"

Tess's hand paused on the dresser drawer. "What?"

"Try to participate today, you know, really get something out of it. Okay?"

She turned with a smirk and forced an upbeat tone, "Of course! I do that every day."

Her mom met the statement with rolled eyes but didn't argue the point any further and walked back into the hallway, closing the door behind her gently.

Tess looked at her clothes. She'd outgrown many of the tight-fitted and trendy outfits she'd worn just earlier this year. Now she mostly sported baggy t-shirts, sweaters, and sweatpants. She moved her gaze to the mirror and met heavy eyes with deep purple bags blooming beneath them. They suggested she hadn't slept for days, while the reality was quite the opposite.

She touched her jaw where acne lined her face worse than she'd ever experienced before. It was scarring her skin. She tried face wash, acne cream, and natural remedies, but nothing worked. It was just an unavoidable side effect of the medication.

She frowned at the girl in the mirror but didn't have the energy to think about her looks any longer. She faced larger hurdles.

As she left the house, Tess checked her phone, unsurprised to find that she had no new notifications. It was the last week of March, and most of her friends wouldn't be returning from college for another month. Until they returned, they were focused on a different life, which she understood. She had friends at her college, but they'd all been bystanders to her life falling apart. She wasn't ready to go back there, talk to those people, or risk seeing her old classmates. She just wanted to pretend like that part of her life never happened.

The drive wasn't bad in the end. The fear seemed to stem more from Tess's imagination than reality, which, she learned last month, was quite vast and perhaps too loud. She parked across the street from a large office building, and then walked toward the entrance.

The building housed a diverse range of businesses. Tess's group therapy was held on the third floor. An older man in a suit walked out as she approached the door, holding it open for her with a smile. She wondered if he would treat her differently if he knew which business she was here for. She entered the empty elevator and hit the third-floor button, beating a rhythm into the hand bar as it rose.

"Hey, girl!" called the young secretary as Tess entered the waiting room. Tess suppressed a groan. This girl was way too happy all the time, and what for?

"Hi." Tess forced a smile and walked through the open door on the other side of the room. It led back to the individual offices and the group room.

She pushed through the first door on her left, then sank into an old armchair next to the window in the left corner of the room.

The group constantly changed, and today, she recognized three of the four participants. She could never remember their names, but she recalled one was a divorced man with anxiety, another a mother suffering from depression, and the last a woman in her thirties who had not specified a diagnosis. Today, they were joined by a fourth man; he looked to be in his late forties. His leg was bouncing up and down, and he nervously scrolled through his phone.

The group had a fast turnover rate, so Tess was a veteran after two weeks. The longer she stayed in the group, the longer she pushed off her individual counseling. So, she stayed. Tess placed her hands underneath her legs, the weight providing enough discomfort to keep her looking attentive. She mentally prepared for another long and torturous session.

This group was mandated for her as outpatient treatment, but she didn't see the point. She wasn't ready to talk about her manic episode. Yet, four lovely days a week, she sat in this group, learned absolutely nothing useful, and pretended to worry about the troubles of parenthood or losing 'the love of your life'.

She had no doubt the hardships were real and valid to the people who presented them, but she also failed to connect them to her own recovery. She wasn't a parent, nor had she come close to being in love.

She closed her eyes to savor the last few seconds of peace before Melinda would come barreling in. And sure enough, that moment lasted only seconds.

"Okayyy! And who do we have here today?!" Her shrill voice filled the room, and she scooted into one of the empty armchairs. Today, she wore a long-sleeved green shirt under a brown V-neck, paired with a bright floral maxi skirt. Her greying brown hair was pulled halfway up with a floral clip holding it together behind her head. The years of her career as a therapist clearly weighed on her wrinkled face as she smiled at Tess. "Tess, great! Oh, and John, Donna, and Marie, wonderful! And now we have Matthew! Matthew, would you like to introduce yourself?"

"Uh...yeah, I'm Matthew. I never...um really did a group before. My mom really pushed for it. She's been worried recently..." His story trailed on, but Tess's gaze turned outside the window. She counted the cars and then sorted them by color.

As he finished, she gauged that he suffered from depression and was dealing with significant stress from a work layoff, as well as some other problems that, at the moment, she couldn't relate to. She closed her eyes.

Problems she couldn't relate to. Then, what was her problem? One day, she'd be working too. Maybe she should pay attention. Soon, she would have to share something. What bothered her?

The white walls. They bothered her. They appeared in her mind frequently. The empty white walls. The nurses that chased her down the hallways, the dropping sensation in her stomach, the running for her life. But she had been trapped by the white walls, the empty white walls. She was suffocating, and soon they would kill her.

She gasped for air and opened her eyes. She wasn't there— not anymore. Instead, she was in this group session listening to various irrelevant problems, with every eye of the group now focused on her, as well, she realized as she returned her gaze to the room.

"Tess, would you like to share next?" Melinda asked in a tone that suggested the only correct answer was 'Yes'. She leaned in toward Tess and a vanilla perfume scent lingered in the air.

They always started Tuesday sessions with a summary of the weekend. Tess learned that if you presented a minor and easily solvable problem, Melinda would move on from you rather quickly. There was no point in delving into the deep stuff here, in front of all these other people, and she generally didn't want to go back there at all.

"Hm…well, this weekend, I mostly played video games. My mom and I went shopping for a little bit, but I got too tired, and we decided to go home. I think a lot of the time, recently, I've been too tired to do things I used to enjoy."

"Okay." Melinda seemed satisfied, she leaned back in her chair and turned to the group. "Is this something that anyone in the group can connect with? Do we have any suggestions?"

The new kid slowly spoke up. "Well, I think it's essential to get sleep. My mother says that my depression is linked to my sleeping and…"

Tess began to zone out again. She had said enough to set him off for a while, she figured, and it wasn't like he was providing some groundbreaking new strategies. She'd been in therapy for depression since the eighth grade, so she figured she'd heard it all at this point.

The rest of the group dragged on. John's ex-wife had a new boyfriend, a fact he discovered using a fake Facebook account to follow her life. Melinda spent some time discussing healthy expectations and boundaries.

Donna's child had been taking up too much of her time, and she started neglecting her own health. Melinda's focus turned to hygiene. The discussion followed through on that same theme for the rest of the session.

Tess spoke when she was addressed and she even gave some good advice, whether it was genuine or not. Eventually, the two hours were up, and she had to try not to sprint out of the building.

On her way home, Tess's thoughts drifted back to college. The decision to withdraw still weighed on her heavily. She wondered how much money she had put herself back in student loans and how much money she had put her family back in medical bills. How could she repay them for what she'd put them through?

Her eyes landed on a sign for the grocery store, and she imagined how her family would feel if she were to cook dinner for them. She could almost see the relief on her mother's face and knew her brother would be excited for a homemade stir-fry. She quickly activated her turn signal and pulled over to the parking lot. Inside, she bought chicken and vegetables, then lugged the grocery bags back to her car.

As she pulled into the driveway, her eyelids became heavy again. She forced them to stay open as she brought the food into the kitchen. She stuffed the entire grocery bag into the fridge between two fast food containers and dragged herself up the stairs. Inside, she collapsed on her bed and fell asleep in moments.

Tess slowly sat up in her bed. The world outside her window had gone dark. She heard a group of boys excitedly shrieking on the other side of her wall. Her bedroom bordered her brother's. She pressed a hand against her pulsing forehead.

That pulsing intensified as she checked her phone. It was seven, way past the time she should have started cooking dinner. Her feet slammed on the carpet as she hurried down the stairs. The smell of cheap pizza wafted through the hall as she approached the kitchen.

"Oh no," she groaned as she walked into the room.

"Tess! Have some pizza, I picked it up on the way home," her mother chirped. She sat at the kitchen table, folding laundry.

"No, no. I was supposed to make the chicken," Tess replied in frustration, walking straight past the pizza box open on the counter toward the fridge.

"The chicken? Um...Tess, are you taking your medication?"
Her mother's voice rang with concern.

Tess clenched her hand into a fist, and she closed her eyes.
This had become her mother's go-to response to anything Tess
said that didn't make sense. She was never given a 'What do you
mean?' or a 'Huh?' ever since she returned from the hospital. It
went straight to 'Tess is batshit crazy without medication'.

"No, actually, I bought some chicken to make for the house
because no one else around here ever wants to fucking cook." She
had tried to say it calmly, but couldn't stop the aggression that
rose in her voice as she spoke.

Her mother's body tensed. She dropped the flannel shirt
she'd been folding and turned her entire body toward Tess.
"That's a really cruel thing to say, Tess. Do you know how busy I
am? When are you planning on getting a job anyway? You've been
sitting around playing video games for the past two weeks."

"I don't know, maybe when I don't have to be in therapy or
asleep for half the day. Maybe then I'll look into it, Mom. How's
that sound?"

Tears formed in Tess's eyes as she spoke. She wanted
nothing more than the energy and stability to hold a job. She
wished she didn't depend on her family for anything, but it was
how things had to be as she recovered. Before her mother could
see the tears, she turned and stormed out of the room.

Across the hallway, in the living room, Tess sat down in
front of her haphazard video game set-up and pushed the power
button. Plugged into the side of her laptop was a detachable
keyboard she'd bought on Facebook Marketplace. On the other
side, a mouse glowed a vibrant red, decked out with extra buttons
made for video games. This, she borrowed from her brother.

Tess took a deep breath and drowned out the sounds of her
household with her heavy headset. DuskCabins began its
automatic launch, and she slightly relaxed at the sound of the
launch screen music. However, it was a short-lived peace, as she
was startled by a notification noise.

She looked at her friends list. It contained three boys she'd
gone to high school with. Back in high school, Tess found herself

drifting from group to group. She never settled into just one
clique, and the hierarchy at her school didn't demand that either.

The three boys were always rushing home to play Destiny
with each other, and she would join in on the fun if she had all
her work done. They played tons of squad games over the
summer together before college began. She hadn't seen them
online in a while—she was certain the boys were busy with their
college semesters. Her friend list also included her younger
brother, who was online, playing solo mode with the friends in his
room.

Her brother had trained her quite a bit when she first came
back from college, but now, with all the game time she'd racked
up, she was the one giving him pointers.

What was unfamiliar on her screen was the invitation
notification in the upper right corner of her friends list. Her brow
furrowed. She hadn't asked anyone to add her, and she normally
played solo games online. Her mouse moved across the gray
social box, and she opened the invite.

BlackLantern has sent you a friend request.

Do you:

Accept   Decline

Chapter Three
Escaping Solo Land

Tess startled. She recognized him as the player she watched yesterday. He had good potential. She could tell his building techniques could use more work, but his strategic thinking was what caught her attention. With a little enhancement, he could measure up with the professionals. She wondered how he even found her. She glanced around her living room as if spy cameras were planted inside, then laughed at her paranoia.

After a deep breath, she clicked 'Accept'. Immediately, BlackLantern sat on her friend list, but he was offline.

"How anticlimactic," she said to herself. Her mouse moved to the start match button, and she dropped into her usual mode, solo.

Wind whipped through Tess's hair as she dove headfirst from the airplane, plummeting toward the ground. She had jumped early, hoping to land near lots of other players. A few towns came into view as she descended and curved her body toward the big city.

Metropolis was her usual destination, where chaos was guaranteed to erupt at the start of every match. She aimed for the northwest corner of the city, heading for her usual spot—a towering apartment building. It had a few places to grab resources, but was often overlooked, since it was sitting closer to the city's outskirts.

Tess's feet struck the apartment building roof with a loud thud, and she jumped onto a concrete balcony below with ease. Her eyes swept the area, locking onto four players clustered centrally around the city's dolphin monument. Two more sprinted toward a pizza shop across the street. There were likely others, but that was enough for a start.

Three wood planks zigzagged, boarding up the path toward the inside of the penthouse. With a few quick swings of her fist, she chopped through them. Stepping into a dimly lit bedroom, her eyes widened with excitement. Lying on the floor in front of her was a golden shotgun.

As she made her way to the lobby, she grabbed a few grenades, ammo, an ordinary assault rifle, and standard armor. She was nearly at the door when an explosion shook the building. A smile tugged at her lips as she turned toward the noise source. She spotted a battle unfolding on the other side of the building through an open window. Without hesitation, she swiped her palm across the wall, and the entire side of the structure vanished.

On the street, two players—one a human-sized raccoon, the other a baseball player—stood at opposite ends, their wooden forts offering little protection. The raccoon peeked his head over a small wooden wall that shielded him from the baseball player. Meanwhile, the baseball player remained crouched down behind his own wall, hurriedly gulping down a purple healing potion.

Tess grabbed her assault rifle and took two quick shots, eliminating the raccoon. Unaware of her position, the baseball player began panicking, building frantically further from where the raccoon had been.

"What a bot," she muttered.

Two easy shots, and he went down as well. Tess didn't bother sorting through their limited supplies. Instead, she turned her attention to the area where she'd seen the other four players land. At the top of the dolphin monument, there was visible explosive damage; his nose hung down by a hinge.

"What, are you guys having all the fun without me?" She laughed and took off toward the center of town.

Usually, Tess would be more cautious at the start of a match, but the golden shotgun gave her all the confidence she needed. She approached a circular building to the left of the monument, with multiple floors and metal pipes sticking out at odd ends.

She stepped slowly into the bottom floor and paused momentarily, listening for the sound of footsteps. One player was at the top, and two were fighting somewhere in between, but where was the fourth?

The game notified her when the other players died, and she hadn't any kills besides her own. So that meant—BAM. The shot fired just as Tess ducked behind a bookshelf. The fourth was down here with her. She pulled out her shotgun, took a deep breath, and popped back up. The other player was still in the same spot, reloading his gun. He was dead before she could even exhale.

The smell of gunpowder overwhelmed her senses as she listened again. There was repeated thudding on the ceiling, as if someone was jumping rope above. Tess reloaded as she walked back out the main entrance, searching for a window that bordered the second floor. She spotted one at the back of the building and quickly built up to it, then peeked inside. Two players circled the room, jumping, dodging, and missing every shot.

She waited for the first to get close, then took her shot, pumping him once with the shotgun. Without waiting to gauge the other player's position, she quickly built a wall between herself and the room. She listened carefully for a moment. Once she knew which direction he approached from, she knocked down her wall and fired a shot. One shot was all she needed. He was dead.

"Wow, I love this golden shotgun." She laughed and began to reload, preparing to face the next player. But in the time she'd spent celebrating, she failed to account for his movements.

The sound of bending metal croaked on her left, and she turned just in time to face a purple magician hanging upside down from a pipe on the exterior of the building. He didn't hesitate to fire a shotgun blast of his own, and her screen faded to black.

Game Over

"That third partying bastard," she cursed as her game returned to the home screen.

"Yeah, I don't fuck with third partying kids either."

She recognized that voice from the previous night.

BlackLantern was sitting in her lobby. She must have missed the notification that he joined her party as she lost herself in the game. She opened her mouth to respond, but no words came out.

She'd been witty and quick with comebacks in the past, but things had changed recently. Her confidence, even the speed of her thoughts. And then this was a conversation over the microphone—something new.

"Uh, hi," she finally managed to say, heat rushing to her face. Why was this so difficult? She'd always had friends when she was in school. She wasn't the most outgoing person, but she was more than capable of holding a conversation.

"So, you're probably wondering why some creepy ass guy found you on DuskCabins and is now sitting in your lobby."

She burst out laughing. Okay, so this wouldn't be so hard. "Me? No, I mean you're creepy-ass guy number three hundred and seven, so you've caught me at a well-adjusted point in my life."

His deep laugh greeted her in return, and some of the tension Tess had held on to all day faded away.

"But uh, I am curious—why did you add me? And how?"

He cleared his throat. "I just check out most of the accounts that hang in my buddy's stream. Your Twitch is connected to DuskCabins, if you didn't know. Most people are looking for carries, attention, or just begging for someone to play with, but you didn't ask for any of that."

She laughed again. "Uh, yeah, so? I'm sure hundreds of people pass through like that. I mean, he played with EFN Perktuns." She paused. Why was she laughing? He hadn't even made a joke. "What makes me so special?"

"Well, when I say I check the players out, I look at their in-game statistics. It might be a pride thing, like I'm making sure my skills are above the viewers. Sometimes it's scouting for my buddy, but your stats...they confused me."

Her stats? She'd honestly never looked them up. She didn't see the point; this game was just a way to waste time until she could return to college. "And what about them? 'This girl is a loser?' 'Spends more time in solo land than Eeoyre?'"

"What?" He sounded genuinely thrown off by her last comment.

"Nothing. It's from a show." She suppressed her laughter. Had he really never watched Winnie the Pooh? What kind of person was this?

"Well, yes...partially. Clearly, from your lack of duo or team games, you're not competing. So that was intriguing. But based on your solo scores...well, you're placing higher than me."

She faked a gasp. "The astonishment! There's a better player than the world-renowned—" she paused to review his username, "...BlackLantern. I mean, bro, I hadn't even heard of you before yesterday. Why should I feel so special to be outplacing you?"

He laughed, but his voice changed when he said, "Maybe because, in the past week, I've made 2000 bucks off the game."

This time, her gasp was real. "Sorry, hold on. You mean to tell me I'm a better player than you?"

There was rustling behind his mic, but eventually his voice came over clear. "Statistically speaking, slightly."

Tess continued, "And you've made 2000 bucks. Meanwhile, I'm sitting over here begging my mom for money to get an iced coffee."

"Well, I mean, I didn't know all that...but yeah, the main idea is the same. Basically, what I'm trying to say is that I compete. I do tournaments, wagers, and I win because I'm good. I've never viewed a DuskCabin's profile with stats as good as yours where the user has never competed in wagers or tournaments. Honestly...I'm astounded. What have you been doing?"

He sounded genuinely intrigued. Intrigued about Tess in a way that had nothing to do with her mental health. In fact, he knew nothing about her; he had no idea what had happened.

He didn't speak to her like she was a vase that had already shattered and was held together by glue, ready to crack again at the sound of the wrong syllable. It was like a breath of fresh air.

"I don't know. I've been watching the good players. I know they compete, but they're on sponsored teams. I've just been playing for fun. I don't have a lot going on right now...and I don't have a lot of people to play with."

She wondered if he would push her to explain why she had so much time or why no one was around, so she started formulating explanations in her head.

To her relief, he breezed right past it. "Well, I'm looking for a duo. Sizzars is my buddy and he's great, but our teamwork...it's sloppy at best. His stats don't nearly match yours either. You wanna run a few games, and see if we work well together?"

"Okay, and if so, then what?"

He laughed, "Then we make bank."

Tess had not been up past two since she began her treatment, but she barely noticed the clock as time flew by tonight. She had the skill; she was always working on it, but under BlackLantern's strategic guidance, she felt like a brand-new player.

She had always preferred to play alone. Even with her friends from high school, she usually felt too frustrated with their decisions to continue playing squad games for too long.

She'd never been able to play with someone whose skill level matched her own. She'd never felt proud of the skill either. It just seemed like proof of the immense amount of time she'd been wasting away while her friends lived out their real lives.

"Alright, I'll get my own assault rifle ammo if you don't want to share," BlackLantern grunted.

"Huh? Oh, sorry. I wasn't listening."

He laughed. He was circling the neighborhood, watching out for any approaching threats. Tess was restocking on health items before they would move on to face the last living duo. She approached BlackLantern and handed over half of her assault rifle ammo.

"Clearly."

"I just noticed how late it is..." Tess continued. It was three in the morning. She was astounded that no one in the house had come to pull her off the game. Although the living room was far away from any bedrooms, it was possible her voice didn't reach them. Or, perhaps, her parents were happy to hear her talking to someone besides herself while playing the game for once.

"Oh, shit! What time zone are you in?"

He actually sounded concerned for her. A small smile formed on her face, but she reminded herself that he only cared because she was his new ticket to winning more money. Which was entirely fair, as that's what he was to her. Right?

"East Coast, hence, why I keep complaining about your West Coast server lag. So, yeah, it's three here."

She wondered how many details about her location she was supposed to give to a stranger on the internet. Although, after all the hours of gameplay, Lantern didn't seem so much like such a stranger. And he certainly did not seem untrustworthy. Then again, she wondered if that thought was naïve. She was still calling the guy 'Lantern' in her mind.

"Ahh, I see...I thought you were just covering for yourself. I know it can be intimidating to play with someone like me." As he spoke, he sprinted ahead, quickly building ramps and platforms in front of him to construct a fast tower.

She began forming a rebuttal, but the words died on her lips because his obnoxious building had attracted attention from the other duo. A sniper shot connected to BlackLantern's head, and he was knocked off his tower and onto the ground.

In duo mode, when one teammate was knocked down, they stayed alive but couldn't take action, leaving the surviving player with a chance to revive them.

His mic was dead silent. Tess burst out into laughter as she instinctively brought walls between her body and the direction of the shot. While she spoke, she worked her way to BlackLantern's body. "I don't know if I would use the word intimidating, but—"

The sound of firing from above cut her off, and she froze. The other duo had moved quickly and were now on a rooftop, well within range.

"Forget me. Finish it out," BlackLantern called.

Tess smiled. That would be no problem for her.

"Don't act so happy about it either! I had more kills than you during the last game," he added.

She laughed, "Yes, one time, out of what—twenty games?" She ducked behind her wall and pulled out a sniper rifle. One shot flew by her left side, targeting BlackLantern, and he vanished, fully eliminated.

She knew where the player had to stand to make that shot. She ducked out from her wall, quickly scoped in on the sniper rifle, and found the player right where she expected. He was knocked down within a second.

She slipped back behind her cover and listened to the knocked player's partner make his way over to his duo. He was going for the revive. She peeked out from the other side of her wall to see that he had built good coverage for his partner and himself. That meant she was going to need to get closer for the kill.

"Well, this is fun," she whispered to herself genuinely.

BlackLantern's quiet laugh startled her for a moment. She was so used to talking to herself while she played that she had almost forgotten he was on the call with her. Swapping her sniper for a shotgun, she started toward the house.

"Throw up some grenades," Lantern reminded her. She didn't respond aloud but reached into her backpack. Her hand gripped a cylindrical object, and she flicked it up toward the building. It exploded against the wall on impact. The living duo had to stop healing their partner to bring the wall back up.

If she hadn't made the move, the other player would have likely finished his revival before she was close enough to the roof to intervene. It would have been two players versus her, which she could still probably win, she thought, smirking, but Lantern was right. It was better this way.

After he built the wall back up, Tess's opponent began to build more ramps up and out toward her instead of turning back to his teammate.

He already had a high vantage point from the roof, and now his position was getting stronger. Tess wasn't bothered; she began to build back and forth below his builds so that they became her new protection. She heard his footsteps above and she circled her own ramp in an upward spiral until she ended up behind his highest platform.

She prepared for his first shot, timing a new wall successfully between the two of them as soon as it was released. Before he could reload, she swiped the wall away, raised her golden shotgun, and landed a clean headshot.

VICTORY: BLACKLANTERN AND JUSTATESST

"You know, I think that should really just say my name," Tess said through a yawn.

"I don't know what you said, but I'm going to assume it was offensive," Lantern replied, then paused.

For a moment there was silence on both ends. Tess wondered if perhaps she should have been a little nicer but frowned. It was hard to be anyone other than herself.

"You should get some sleep," he continued.

She was somewhat disappointed to hear him say that. One part of her was ready to keep this streak going, but simultaneously, she could feel the adrenaline mask fading and her fatigue setting in.

"Yeah, you're right. So, uh...about being duos...I don't know...I thought maybe we played well...I mean, I don't know what your other duos have been like..."

Her face was turning red again. She knew she was good, and she thought they played well together, but she didn't realize how much she would just enjoy playing with the guy, for free. It wasn't just the money she stood to lose if he didn't want to become a duo.

His voice came back measured and careful. He seemed to pick up on her anxiety, which she scolded herself for. She hoped he didn't think she was hesitant. She wasn't apprehensive at all, just more guarded. Vulnerability like this didn't exist in her world of solo matches.

"Yeah, I think just about after the six-game victory streak, I knew I found a new duo," he replied.

That was hours ago. So why did he keep her wondering for so long? Still, she was glad he did; it pushed her to give her all in these games and made them even more fun.

"Thank God...I can't wait to afford coffee again."

Money was, of course, the entire point of this arrangement. But she couldn't help wondering if he picked up on the desperation buried beneath her words. Ugh, she had to get out of here. She was starting to sound pathetic, even to herself.

"Gotta sleep. Same time tomorrow?"

"Yep, that can be arranged. Goodnight, Tess."

"Goodnight...uh, Lantern?"

He laughed, "Cade."

"Night, Cade."

Without waiting for a response, she closed the game. A grin spread across her face as she glanced around the room. It had gone completely dark, illuminated only by the faint glow of her laptop screen. She let out a deep breath and powered it down.

She dragged herself up the stairs, took her five pills and crawled into bed. Sleep claimed her quickly, as it always did. It was silent, heavy, and dreamless.

But for the first time since the hospital, she had something exciting to anticipate for the next day. She just hoped it was around to stay.

Chapter Four
The Girl Before

Tess cracked two eggs into a bowl as she prepared breakfast for herself. She stirred the mixture and poured it into the pan. As it dropped onto the steel surface it sizzled, and the scent of butter quickly filled the air. Beside the oven, her laptop sat on the counter, playing a highlight video from EFN Perktuns's tournament game. As the eggs cooked, her gaze flicked between the stove and the stream, her mind trying to absorb the strategy.

"What has gotten into you?"

Tess paused the video and turned to see her mother standing in the kitchen doorway, one arm on her hip. In the other hand, her mother held Tess's water glass, no doubt to refill it ahead of schedule for the night.

"What? I've made eggs before," Tess said, turning back to the stove, attempting to keep her voice nonchalant.

She knew exactly what her mother was implying, but she didn't think waking up early to cook breakfast called for a grand celebration.

"Yes, I know you've made eggs before. You did a lot of things *before*."

Tess flinched at the sharp emphasis.

She knew her mother was simply trying to point out a positive; she had started doing something healthy again, something she had stopped doing after her episode. That was good, and cooking was important, but at the same time, she hated to compare herself to who she was before.

For a while after the hospital, she was searching, trying to once again be the same girl that she was before. But after some time, she realized people were not meant to experience such hardships and come out of them unchanged.

"I'm just glad, that's all. It's good to see you up before me."

Tess shook off her initial reaction and decided to accept the praise. She moved her eggs to a plate and replied, "It feels good to be up. I'm excited for the day."

Her mother's face twisted in confusion, and Tess stifled a laugh. She sincerely hoped her mother wouldn't ask if she'd been taking her medication again. Honestly, the words felt so foreign to her own mouth that she couldn't blame her if the question did arise.

"Your sarcasm is getting drier and drier. It's hard for my heart," her mother joked.

Tess laughed. "It's not sarcasm. Really!" She walked over to the island in the center of the kitchen, sat on a stool, and started eating. However, her mother stood frozen in the doorway, concern etched across her face. "You know the game I play? DuskCabins?"

"Yes, well, I know you play some game, but I don't know much else about it."

"Well, the game is online and multiplayer. The best players make enough money for a living just by playing the game. They play for Esports leagues."

Her mother's brow furrowed.

"Think of it like playing for an NFL team or something. Anyway," Tess continued, her voice rising with enthusiasm, "I met someone yesterday. He's at a skill level similar to mine and made thousands of dollars competing. We're going to start competing together." Tess consciously lowered her voice as she finished, realizing her excitement might set off her mother's worry.

"You met him? Oh…is that who you were talking to? Is he in your group therapy? It sounded like you were having an awful lot of fun."

Tess ducked her head as her cheeks burned red.

She hadn't realized that her parents had been listening in on her gaming session. The thought made her stomach twist. She definitely didn't feel like explaining how she met Cade—not when it would trigger a full-blown, outdated stranger-danger lecture, especially from someone who needed help just to post on her Facebook account.

"He's a friend of a friend," she said simply.

"Well, that's good."

Her mother moved to the sink and filled her glass of water. Before leaving the room, she turned back to Tess with a cautious smile.

"You're not worried you're having too much fun?" She seemed to consider whether or not to say the next part, then quietly added, "Like before the hospital?"

"No," Tess replied firmly.

"Okay. I hope this positive mindset lasts for you." Her mother smiled again, but Tess couldn't help noticing the unease behind it. As soon as she left the room, Tess sighed heavily.

It felt like her mother was more apprehensive of her happiness than genuinely excited about the new opportunity. Tess understood why. Her mother had every reason to be cautious, but she had hoped the mention of money might have excited her. Then again, getting excited about something you didn't fully understand was hard.

Even Tess didn't fully grasp the money that could be made. Thousands of dollars just for competing online? It was hard to imagine that kind of money. It was a lot more than she had ever made pushing carts at the local grocery store.

She pushed play on the highlights video again and took mental notes as she finished breakfast.

Tess was the second person to arrive at her group later that morning. Bald guy was already seated on his usual couch cushion, probably hoping the divorced mom would sit on the other side,

Tess thought with a laugh. She smirked at the thought of the two of them getting together.

Bald guy caught her gaze and responded with a genuine, toothy smile. Guilt pricked at her. It didn't feel great to make fun of him, even if he couldn't hear. She glanced away quickly.

The room filled within the next few minutes until they were just waiting for Melinda.

"Okayyy! And who do we have here today?!" Melinda sang as she glided into the room. Somehow, she had perfected her consistency in the delivery of this line. It started sounding more like a pre-recorded audio clip than a genuine greeting.

"John, Donna, Tess, and Matthew, wonderful! Let's do a quick check-in on our highs and lows for yesterday. John, why don't we start with you?"

John had his favorite dinner yesterday. He felt sad that it was alone. Donna set aside time to paint her nails. She received an email stating that her daughter was disrupting the classroom. Matthew felt depressed yesterday. He couldn't think of a high.

Melinda reminded the group that it was okay not to have a high, and in that case, it's a good opportunity to think of something you enjoy that you can intentionally add to your schedule. Finally, it was Tess's turn. She had been trying to stay present, but her mind kept wandering back to last night's DuskCabins game.

"I made a new friend yesterday," Tess began. Usually, she would have left it at that, but something compelled her to keep going. "He plays the same video game I do. I'm pretty good at it, and so is he, so we might try competing together."

Her mind returned to last night, specifically to the moment he had tried to show off and outbuild her, only to be immediately shot down by the other team. She couldn't help the grin that spread across her face.

"Well, that's just amazing!" Melinda said, her tone measured but enthusiastic. Tess could tell she was attempting to contain her excitement. This had to be the most Tess had ever contributed at a single time. "And what do you like about the game?"

"I don't know really, I was just playing it to pass the time. Life has felt slow during this recovery process, but..."

She glanced around the room. Everyone watched her with careful anticipation. She still had not shared with this group what she had been through. She still had not shared aloud what she had been through. She still tried not to think about what she had been through.

Her thoughts took her back to the dark hospital hallway. Clues hung around the place, the patients; they were all just one big test, the whole thing; it was just one confusing escape room. Why were they trapping her? Why didn't the clues add up? She laid on the ground for hours, trying to decode messages until she sobbed so hard she couldn't read them anymore. Why wouldn't they let her out?

"...but?" Melinda's voice echoed, twisting down the hallway, and Tess jolted back to the present. In the group room, everyone was watching her with intent. She blinked and then forced a smile.

"But it might be a good outlet for me after all."

She knew this was the kind of answer Melinda wanted to hear. It was safe, something that others could build on, and thus, her contribution time could come to an end.

Tess's assumption was confirmed as Melinda smiled and pivoted her body toward the group. "We can find healthy outlets in many ways! I think that's a great thing to focus on for a little bit today..."

Tess sank back into her chair. She wondered if that had been the right moment to open up about why she was here, what landed her in this group. However, as Matthew and John began discussing their outlets, she decided it wasn't.

This wasn't the place for that story. Here, she could talk about relatable struggles—issues with family and friends, things people could nod along to. But what had happened to her? That didn't feel welcome.

She stared out the window, letting their voices fade into the background. Her thoughts shifted back to DuskCabins, running through strategies for tonight's game. She had a good feeling about it. She just had to make it to tonight.

Chapter Five
Affording Coffee

Tess practically sped home from therapy, bypassing the kitchen entirely, and landed in her computer chair. Her game loaded up, and she untensed seeing Cade's online status. He was also ready. His profile indicated that he had recently started a solo game, so she dove into her own.

Her game dwindled down to the last five players when a notification popped up. Cade had joined her party back in the lobby. In DuskCabins, the map gradually shrinks into a small circle, forcing the remaining players to confront each other. Tess's game had reached the final zone, and her loadout was solid. She decided to see it through before backing out to talk to him.

Three minutes later, she grinned at the victory message on her screen and backed out into the lobby, where Cade was waiting.

"Yo," Tess said, opting for something simpler than: 'Hey, I've been obsessively studying this game all day to improve, and now I'm so excited to play with you again'.

"Wassup?" he responded.

She wondered if that was a simpler way of saying something more complicated on his mind.

"Not much. Just ready to start affording coffee."

He laughed, "Alright, I'm signing us up for a tournament that starts at four. You just need to sign up for an account on the website. I'll text you the link."

She froze for a second. Was he asking for her phone number?

"If that's alright," he quickly added.

She laughed defensively, "Yeah, of course." If she trusted him enough to gamble money on the game, why not her phone number? What was the worst thing that could happen if things went south—she would need to block him?

She rattled off her number, and soon after, a text popped up with a link to the tournament website. Tess followed the steps to sign up and added her username to the site. Afterward, Cade set up their team from his computer and registered them for the tournament.

"Does it cost money to enter?" Tess asked.

"Of course, they use that money to set up the prizes."

"Alright...do you use Cash App?"

He laughed in a way that made Tess feel he knew something that she didn't.

"You don't need to pay me."

Her body tensed slightly. What did he think because of all her coffee jokes, she was living in a cardboard box? A large part of her integrity was wrapped up in being able to provide for herself. It was something she'd lost control of during her hospital stay, and she wasn't about to let that happen again.

"I might not need to pay you," she replied, her tone sharper than intended, "but I don't need to owe you anything either. I can pay for myself, and I can take care of myself."

"Woah, woah, I wasn't trying to imply all that. I just mean I can cover it...because I'm pulling you into this for the first time. I feel it's right I invest in our team for our first tournament. It was my idea, after all." His voice softened as he explained, and Tess exhaled slowly, the tension leaving her shoulders.

She felt a sense of embarrassment at her outburst. Goddammit, she thought, one day, and she'd already pushed the guy away.

"Of course," Cade added, his tone lightening, "if your ass gets us killed. I'll text you over my Venmo."

Tess forgot about the embarrassment as she started laughing, "If anyone's getting us killed, I have a feeling it will be the guy that builds straight up just to stand there and run his mouth."

He was silent for a moment. She wondered if she had gone too far. She tried to imagine his expression, but it was hard to construct the expression without the face.

The moment passed, and he said quietly, "We don't need to bring that up again."

And then they were both laughing.

Tess clicked the ready button in the corner of her screen, and Cade silently followed. Their conversation turned to strategy and what they had been watching on Twitch lately.

They played game after game, experimenting with different strategies—some were working, others not. Tess hadn't played with many other people before, so she didn't have a lot of players to compare Cade to, but she never imagined she'd find such perfect battle chemistry with anyone.

They were pulling off high-kill games consistently, and Tess knew she'd been performing well on her own before, but the effectiveness of their duo was taking things to a whole new level.

"Fuck," Cade muttered.

Tess grabbed her shotgun and ran across the abandoned movie theater toward him. She was jumping as she moved to make herself a more challenging target, scanning the room for whatever he must have seen. Popcorn crunched underneath her feet.

"What is it?"

"We've gotta back out. The tournament's in ten minutes."

"Oh shit," she replied as she glanced down at the time at the bottom of her screen. "Alright, let's do it."

Their in-game characters faded out of view, and the screen returned to the game lobby.

"We'll join with the two people we're competing against, then play separately as two duos. Whichever pair ends up with more kills gets to proceed to the next round."

"How many teams do we need to beat?"

"Four teams until the final game. After that, the winner takes the entire two-thousand-dollar pot."

Tess felt a flutter of nerves, but the high stakes added a numbness that dulled it. She couldn't quite picture herself making that much money in a single night. It felt distant like it wasn't truly on the line.

"Should I add the players to my friend's list?" she asked.

"No, I'll add them. You never know what kind of people they will be. I wouldn't want you to be stuck with them on your list."

Was he trying to protect her? A warmth spread across her body, a feeling of safety. It was weird how someone she didn't truly know could make her feel that way.

They sat in the lobby, waiting for their first two opponents to join. They'd gone over their strategy, but now, with the topic of the game covered, Tess wondered what else she could talk about. She racked her brain for a topic, anything that wasn't related to her mental health but still felt more meaningful than DuskCabins.

"Damn, this is harder work than a high-kill game."

Tess tried not to slap herself in the face as she realized the words had escaped her lips. She had a bad habit of talking to herself. It wasn't really a problem when she was playing games alone, daydreaming, or arguing with nobody in the shower. But in a situation where she'd just met someone she got along with and might even be able to start earning an income with, that's when it became a problem.

Cade laughed. "I'm not good at sitting still either."

She smiled. It wasn't exactly what she had meant, but it was definitely something they had in common.

"What great things happen to people that sit still anyway?" Tess posed, trying to keep the tone light.

"They get a great nine-to-five with an average income and feel content," he responded quickly as if the thought had crossed his mind before

Tess felt that deeply. It was the path she was on—or, more accurately, the one she had been pushed toward before everything happened.

The idea of 'college or no future' had been force-fed to her from the time she was a kid. Now, here she was, a year and a half into debt that she could only afford to pay off if she finished her degree. She was supposed to go back after the break from this semester.

Cade didn't sound like he'd bought into the whole college thing. In fact, she knew he hadn't based on the time in the West Coast and the fact that it was a weekday. He wasn't stuck at an office desk somewhere, nor was he sitting in a classroom.

"What, do you work a five-to-one and feel ecstatic?" she asked, half teasing, half serious.

"God no, who wakes up that early?" Cade laughed. He was right; Tess had just picked a random time off the top of her head. "My work hours are…flexible."

"That's nice," Tess said quietly, "my school hours too."

"What's up? What's up?" a new voice rang through the headset.

Two new players had joined the lobby. Tess had to turn down the volume on her headset to combat the static sound coming from one of their microphones. The player who had spoken sounded prepubescent, and the other player was silent.

"You guys ready?" Cade asked.

"You know it," that same player responded.

"Alright."

The blue lobby faded, and the screen turned to a dark purple. It read tournament mode. The four players stood as one group below the text at first, but slowly, the two duos moved to opposite ends of the screen.

As they moved, the microphones cut out so the players could only hear their partners. Tess's screen asked if it was okay to record her progress and send it back to the tournament website. She checked yes. Within moments, they were riding in an airplane, approaching the map.

The games went by in a blur. The first few victories were expected, but Tess began to feel the pressure mounting as they advanced further into the bracket. Cade, on the other hand, seemed to thrive under it, and he kept her grounded.

"Pretend it's any other practice game we've played…you just want to win, like always," he kept reminding her.

Everyone in the house had wisely avoided Tess, allowing her to stay in the zone while she played, far from the complicated, dreary world around her.

Tess let herself exhale after a close ending to their semi-final match. They'd only pulled ahead by one kill in the end. She stared at the screen as they reported their scores to the website and waited to find out who they would face in the finals.

"Cade, I think I might be dying," Tess said, only half joking as breathing had literally begun to occur less often for her. Her knuckles turned white as she gripped onto the sides of the folding chair stationed in her living room.

Cade laughed, but his voice was calm. "You're doing great, Tess! Just try to stay in the moment. I'm sick of carrying the team."

Tess practically forgot her own anxiety at the comment. Her vision went red. "HOLD ON. Who had more kills in the last match? And what do you even think you were—Oh I see what you're doing."

He feigned innocence, his tone light. "I don't know what you mean."

Tess crossed her arms. "You're trying to make me so angry that I forget how terrified I am for this match."

"Is that so?" His voice was playful. "Is it working?"

She frowned. It was working—so well it annoyed her. How could someone she had only met a few days ago manage to push her buttons with such ease? She wished there was someone like Cade around in real life. He was so far removed from her life outside the game that he didn't feel like a real person.

He dropped the act and chuckled. "You just make it so easy to set you off."

"Well, you're so annoying; it doesn't take much effort," she teased.

"How did some dude and his girlfriend make it to the end of the tournament bracket?" A new deep voice bellowed through her headset.

Tess felt her face go red. A million ways to deny what had just been said ran through her mind, but she struggled to settle on a single phrase to actually leave her lips.

She hadn't noticed the two players join their lobby, and now she wondered how much of the conversation they had heard.

"You sick of carrying this chump, honey?" A much more high-pitched, squeaky voice chimed in.

Tess cringed at the word honey. This was precisely why she stayed in solo land. Strangers on video games were always making off-putting comments. Whether she played with random teammates or in tournaments, it didn't seem to matter.

Up until now, Tess had let Cade handle all the talking. Whether Cade noticed Tess's silence or not, he hadn't teased her. It seemed like he knew when to draw the line. Tess's heart beat a little faster at the thought that maybe some protective part of him didn't want her talking to those guys. Her mind wandered into the fantasy, indulging the idea since he had firmly discouraged her from adding them to her list.

"Listen, can you guys stop throwing yourself at my teammate and ready up so she can kick your ass please?" Cade said.

Tess smiled but refused to give the guys any more attention from her voice. She would let her gameplay do the talking.

Her gameplay spoke volumes. The match had simmered down to eight players including Tess, Cade, and their tournament opponents. Tess and Cade held the lead with a combined twelve kills, but their teammates weren't far behind with eleven. They needed two more kills to secure the victory.

Like always, the map was shrinking, and now the only areas left to fight within were the lake house, desert, and river.

"I'm rotating to the lake house. You take the desert and the river," Cade instructed as he peered at the closing zone from a hill.

Tess thrived in open areas where she could build her own ramps to control the flow of the fight. On the other hand, Cade performed better with pre-existing structures, where he could focus on his strategic positioning.

"Sir, yes sir," she joked and threw her hands into a salute. She stood right behind him, watching his back. Her heart thundered, but the humor kept her mind grounded.

He dropped from the hill and started sprinting for the lake house. A rustling sounded in the distance. Tess instinctively waved her arm, generating four walls around herself. Peeking through the top, she spotted two players running across the river, building platforms as they walked across.

Her body tensed, and she prepared her shotgun for a quick attack. Then, she noticed their tournament opponents emerging from a hedge maze on the opposite side of the river. They were moving in with the same plan. Tess's mind raced. If she waited to get close for the attack, it might already be too late.

"There's two on their way here, but the other guys are on them," Tess informed Cade.

"I'm looking for the other two. You need to steal those kills!" Cade urged.

Tess tossed the shotgun over her shoulder and pulled out her sniper rifle. With a quick wave of her arm, she built ramps leading her to a higher vantage point. Now, she just needed to wait for the perfect shot.

Her opponents closed in on the river, laying in with assault rifle shots. This was precisely what Tess had been waiting for. The duo inside the river froze and then turned to her opponents. They began building cover from the incoming shots but overlooked one critical detail: Tess's position.

She pressed the sniper rifle scope to her eye, adjusting her aim just slightly above one of the player's heads. She took a breath, then pulled the trigger. The shot rang out, and the player dropped instantly.

"I knocked one of the players," Tess called to Cade.

"That's my girl," Cade replied with approval.

Tess could barely contain how her heart fluttered at the words, but she had to. There was more to be done before they would win.

The downed player's partner was in a panic. He began
building walls around him in every direction, enclosing his
teammate. There was no doubt he was hoping to revive him.

She sprayed down the wall in front of her, but the player in
the river was quick, rebuilding it as soon as it fell. It left no time
for another shot. Tess's hands shook with the pressure as she
stopped to reload her sniper rifle.

"Got one!" Cade's voice echoed in her headset. "He's
finished off completely. Just make sure the knocked player dies
before he can be revived."

Relief flooded through Tess, but she didn't have time to
savor it. With a deep breath, she jumped out of her tower and
started sprinting through tall grass toward the river. Her heart
pounded with the rush of the game. She could see the last player
desperately trying to revive his teammate, but she wouldn't let that
happen.

Her opponents had backed off into the hedge maze, trying
to give the knocked player a chance at being revived. Afterward,
they could swoop in for both kills. Whereas if the knocked player
died without a revival, Tess would get credit for the elimination,
and that would be the game.

As she sprinted, she pulled out her assault rifle and unloaded
on the wall in front of her. It shattered instantly, revealing the
remaining player hurriedly wrapping bandages around his
teammate's leg. Without hesitation, Tess sprayed her gun at the
medic, and he was decimated in three quick shots. As the last of
his health evaporated, his teammate, who was still knocked,
followed him into the void.

"We won!" Tess exclaimed, breathless and buzzing with
adrenaline.

Cade finished off the last opponent, and the match officially
ended. The two were quickly sent back to the lobby. They backed
out quickly before the losing team could unleash their complaints.

"Good shit, Tess!" Cade cheered. "Send me your Venmo."

"Oh my god! I can't believe we won!"

"Focus, Tess," Cade laughed on the other end.

She quickly texted over her Venmo username, hands shaking as she pressed each letter.

A few moments later, her phone buzzed. Victory was the memo, and $1,000 was the content. Tess thought she might faint.

"And all this time, you were a brunette in my head," Cade teased.

The fainting sensation intensified. She'd forgotten entirely that her Venmo had a profile picture.

Wait...that meant that—she opened Cade's Venmo profile.

"And I thought you were blonde," she breathed out.

He was brunette, tan, young, and cute. She hadn't really thought he was blonde, but she just wanted to throw something back at him. She'd never really pictured him as a real person. Now, she realized just how real he was.

Her eyes moved over to his recent transactions, but his account was private. Her curiosity burned, but she quickly snapped out of it. She was starting to feel like she was crossing some boundary she wasn't meant to.

"That tournament was too easy," Cade said. "I think we should finish the night by reinvesting what we've won in some wager games."

"Sounds good."

Tess let out a quiet sigh of relief. She didn't know why, but she was glad he had brought the focus back to something familiar. The tension had been building, and his casual tone made it feel like nothing had changed. Yet, something in her mind argued instead that everything had changed.

Chapter Six
Graduation

"Today is a special day for the group," Melinda said in her sing-song voice.

A statement like that once would have put Tess on edge, but today, she shared Melinda's excitement. She was ending her sentence of outpatient group therapy and moving on to individual counseling. It was mid-April, and she finally decided to take the initiative to move forward with her treatment plan.

"Tess has been one of our longest and dearest members."

She had to contain her laughter at the word dearest. It was ironic, given Tess had bullshitted her way through most of her contributions, barely listened to what other people shared, and recycled the same advice she had read in depression pamphlets since she was a teenager.

"...but she is ready to move on from the group."

Tess met Melinda's gaze and held it for a moment. That simple act wasn't easy for her. She felt so much sensitivity in someone else's gaze. There was something incredibly vulnerable about people's eyes and altogether too revealing; she always needed to glance away.

But at this moment, Tess fought the discomfort so she could absorb the genuine pride radiating from Melinda's expression. It wasn't just pride in the fact that Tess was ready to move on and work through her manic episode; it was pride in Tess herself.

Tess suddenly realized Melinda likely knew how she held back in these group sessions. Yet, she never pushed Tess to share anything she wasn't ready to discuss. For the first time, Tess felt a deep appreciation for the counselor. Maybe she would even miss her.

"Do you have any last thoughts you want to share with the group?" Melinda asked gently.

Tess hesitated. She knew this was coming; Melinda asked everyone the same question when they left. And yet, despite it crossing her mind more than once, she still had no answer.

"I guess what I would say is…" Tess scoured her brain, flipping through mental health tips she'd read over the years, but none of them felt right. Everyone was watching her, waiting. She didn't know what to say, so she just started speaking.

"I think something I've learned from this group, and from all my mental health experiences in general, is…you can take your meds, sit in therapy, watch your hygiene, make routines, and follow all those 'perfect life' self-help books. But if you're not ready to be honest with yourself and to dig into your deeper feelings, emotions, and trauma, you're going to be sitting at a standstill with your mental health.

"I overstayed my welcome in this group because I was scared to move forward and face some of what I've been through. I got comfortable in my standstill. But things have been changing in my life, and I want more for myself. I know I have to follow my own advice to keep improving, and I hope everyone here finds a way to do that for themselves, too."

Warm tears slipped down Tess's cheeks as she breathed the last words. She hesitated to scan the room, shocked at how much had spilled out of her. But after a moment, she glanced up. The room was filled with knowing nods and sympathetic smiles.

She wiped the tears from her cheeks and sat back in the armchair. A wave of guilt washed over her. She'd been so quick to pass judgment in every session and dismiss other people's vulnerability without even knowing what it felt like to share from the heart.

"That's incredible advice, Tess. I am so glad you have learned such a valuable lesson here." Melinda didn't speak in her usual sing-song tone. Her voice was soft, serious. "I wish you the best of luck in all your future endeavors."

And just like that, the session was over. The room emptied, and Tess followed, her steps slower than the rest. As the group filed out of the office, she lingered behind, her hand trailing down the cool railing as she descended the stairs. The spring air felt crisp outside as she headed to her car.

When she arrived home, Tess collapsed into bed. The fatigue from her medication still hit her hard, and she needed her energy recharged for her nightly gaming with Cade. They had continued success since the first tournament. Tess had earned enough prize money to build her own custom PC, which enhanced her gameplay even more. Now, she upgraded from gaming in the living room to a desk in her bedroom.

The rest of her winnings went straight to savings. She wanted to pay her parents back for all the medical bills they'd covered and start chipping away at her student loans. The situation was more than ideal. Tess was making more than she ever could at a part-time job while still keeping up with her outpatient treatment.

Her parents were thrilled with how things were turning out, though they didn't fully understand what she was doing or exactly how much money she'd been making. She was holding out on that information until she could write them a large check.

Cade: Wake up, sleeping beauty. We have tournaments to win.

The chime of her phone abruptly startled Tess awake later that evening. She grinned at Cade's text. He always teased her about her pre-game naps, but he never pressed her about why she was constantly tired. And she loved that about him.

Cade didn't know anything about her outpatient treatment, her mental health struggles, or the meds that kept her afloat but left her drained. Sometimes, the secret felt like a barrier between them, something she should share with him or that she was supposed to announce about herself. He didn't seem like the type to really judge her either, but she enjoyed having a relationship where her mental health wasn't so central, where it was irrelevant, as far as he knew.

Tess: Alright, Alright, I'm up. The hard carry is coming. Just need to eat.

She smirked at the text as she imagined Cade's reaction to 'the hard carry'. In reality, they were equally dependent on each other during the tournaments; no one was really doing the 'carrying', but teasing him always felt fun.

The thought of seeing his live reaction tugged at her heart. She wished she could be there, in person, to shove him playfully. She could picture his dimples forming, just like in his Venmo picture.

"Ohhhhhh my god, I am pathetic…" she sighed as she headed to the kitchen.

"What, Tess?" her mother called, peering through the kitchen doorway, looking up the stairs.

"Nothing!"

Inside the kitchen, Tess inspected a pan on top of the oven and discovered her mother had prepared some vegetables with chicken. She grabbed a plate and began loading it up. "This looks great, Mom. Thanks."

"Oh, good. You like it? Your dad will never eat those vegetables, but I love them," her mom said with a laugh.

Tess smiled, knowing it was true; her dad would never touch anything green.

"What are you doing tonight?" her mother asked.

Tess opened her mouth to respond, but her mom quickly added, "Oh wait—let me guess…playing Duck Cabins with Cade?"

Tess didn't bother correcting her on the game title. "Yes and making some money while we're at it."

"Well, I can believe that after seeing that new computer of yours."

Something in her mother's voice sounded careful, as though she tiptoed toward something Tess wouldn't want to hear. Tess started racking through all the possibilities in her head, which quickly brought forth a headache.

"And I'm glad those tournaments are going well…"

Her mother was approaching the real question so slowly that Tess's mind kept wandering, until she felt like she was falling through the ground, just like Alice on her way to Wonderland. She wished her mother would just get to her point.

"Mom, stop tiptoeing! You're giving me a headache," Tess blurted out, exasperated.

"What?" Her mother sounded sincerely lost.

Tess could understand why, but she had no patience to explain.

"Never mind…it just seems like you are trying to say something—so get to the point."

Tess watched her mother's furrowed brow fade, and her expression returned to her initial apprehension.

"I'm happy you are doing much better, Tess…but I'm worried."

Tess rolled her eyes and sat down at the table with her plate. When was her mother not worried? This felt like the beginning of a long lecture, so she figured she might as well have dinner with the show.

"I'm worried that your progress depends on this game…and this boy. I want to know that if something were to happen…if he hurt you, or if your success in the game changed, you'd still be on the right track."

"Cade wouldn't hurt me," Tess countered, dropping her fork and narrowing her eyes at her mother.

Why did her mom have to villainize someone she didn't even know?

"Getting hurt by the people you least expect is an even deeper cut and—"

"Either way, my recovery is something that is only bound to me. Sure, meeting Cade and playing in these tournaments has given me purpose again, something to look forward to. But no matter what happens with him or the tournaments, the work that

I've started to put into my mental health is separate from all that. With or without Cade, I'll keep taking care of myself."

Her mother seemed satisfied with the answer, so Tess returned to her meal.

"I am so happy to hear that. Dad and I are really proud of you. You know we love you—"

"Mom, I'm trying to eat, not throw up. Thanks," Tess interjected, but she couldn't hide the smile and comfort she felt in her mother's words.

"Oh my god! You are impossible. I can't believe this boy even wants to play with you."

She may have presented the sentence with playful anger, but her shoulders relaxed, and a smile unfolded on her face. Tess rolled her eyes, but truthfully, she couldn't believe it either. Just then, her phone buzzed.

Cade: What is this, a six-course meal? Come onnnn

Tess smiled. It felt good to be wanted.

Tess: It's actually an eight-course meal. We're currently eating salads (course two). Should be two more hours.

"Is that him? Is he cute?"

Her mother walked up behind her, trying to peer over her shoulders at the phone like a gopher popping up and down from its hole. Tess glared at her mother. Of course she'd ask that.

"What? It's just a question," her mom said, her voice innocent, but Tess could hear a subtle, playful tone.

She waved her mother away. Her phone buzzed again.

Cade: Get your sarcastic ass ONLINE.

Tess finished her plate and headed back to her PC. She jumped into a voice call with Cade and launched DuskCabins.

"Today is going to be a great day," he insisted.

At the game's launch, every little problem, concern, and anxiety melted away. It was just her, him, and the frequency waves that carried their conversation. He had so much energy. He always did, and Tess didn't know when he slept to provide it all. It seemed like he was always online.

"Oh, really? And why's that?" she asked, the curiosity in her voice laced with a playful edge.

"Have you heard of the Grand Championship?" he asked.

She had. It was one of the biggest Esports events in the United States, with tournaments for every competitive video game and prize pools that only microtransactions could support.

"Of course," she replied, her voice cautious. She wasn't sure about where he was going with this.

"Today, they announced a series of public DuskCabins tournaments. Anyone can enter. You don't need to be on a professional team. If we place in the top twenty in any tournament in the coming weeks, they'll pay us to travel to New York and compete at the Grand Championship. The DuskCabins prize pool is five million dollars."

Tess sat up in her seat. "Oh my god, Cade, that's insane! You don't think we could really...I mean, there are huge, trained Esport duos out there...surely they will take all the spots."

She couldn't complete a single thought. Her mind just kept bouncing back to the idea of five million dollars. Three weeks ago, having a couple thousand dollars was beyond her mental capacity. But that kind of money? It was a whole new realm beyond what she could imagine.

"We're just as good as them. Trust, I have been studying the statistics. We just need to treat this like any other tournament we've been killing, and we could easily qualify."

Tess went quiet. The fact that they had a chance astounded her.

"And I can see those blue eyes up close."

She dove deeper into that silence, but it was drowned out by her pounding heart. She wanted to say something, anything—she wanted to tell him she'd love to see him too. But any flirtatious response was stuck in her throat.

Instead, she eventually responded, "Only if you start improving that KDA."

God, why couldn't she say anything remotely vulnerable? Cade laughed, but Tess couldn't shake the feeling that she had disappointed him. Either way, they needed to start warming up, and the game consumed them both.

Chapter Seven
Friends and Buddies

The absence of daily groups was a weird adjustment for Tess, but she enjoyed the extra time. She divvied it up between researching DuskCabins strategies on Twitch, solo practice, and additional duo practice with Cade.

After enduring a lecture from her father about getting off screens occasionally, she added an afternoon walk to her routine. Her dad often joined her, and he seemed surprisingly receptive when Tess described the Grand Championship to him. It was surprising because her father had always been a realist. Perhaps, with the income Tess was generating, it was hard to deny the game was yielding tangible financial results.

The first official Grand Championship tournament, scheduled for Saturday, was just around the corner. To prepare, Tess and Cade had been competing in nightly tournaments. They won often, though not without hitting rough patches they could learn from. Tess anticipated even stiffer competition in the upcoming Grand Championship qualifier.

"How did you meet Cade?" her father asked during their walk on Friday afternoon.

Tess found it amusing that her parents were on a first-name basis with Cade, although they hadn't spoken to him themselves. She and her father strolled side by side through their suburban neighborhood. With spring's arrival, the weather warmed, and flowers began to peek through the neighbor's bushes.

"He found me online through my in-game stats," she explained. "He was already competing solo at the time."

Tess didn't feel the need to lie anymore. Cade had proven himself to be trustworthy.

"And you trusted him just like that?" Her father didn't bother hiding his surprise. He pulled his gaze away from a bluejay sitting in a large oak tree to look at Tess.

"Well, no…" Tess brushed off the reaction and smirked as she thought about how she would frame her answer. "First, I had him prove his skills to me." She enjoyed telling the story that way, even if it wasn't entirely true.

"I mean as a person." Her father's tone was far less amused than she'd hoped.

Tess sighed. Her parents' constant questions about Cade's character were wearing her thin. She understood that they were looking out for her, but she'd grown tired of the stranger-danger lectures. She and Cade texted regularly and talked on voice calls every night while gaming. If there were any red flags, she would've noticed them by now.

She steadied her gaze on a dandelion poking through the sidewalk up ahead. "I took normal precautions."

"Well, it's lucky he found you."

She smiled. It was luckier than her father realized. One more week of tournaments, and she'd have enough to repay her parents for her medical expenses.

Their neighbor Donna stood outside her front porch, trimming down bushes with large clippers in hand. She gave them a friendly smile as they passed, and they returned a wave. They continued the walk in silence, the melody of birds and the breeze accompanying them.

After some time, her father asked, "How's therapy going?"

Tess sighed again. Even though she had had a great final session with her group, she was apprehensive about the individual counseling.

"I have my first appointment next Tuesday."

"That's good. And what about your medications?"

"What about them?" she asked, her tone edging toward defensiveness. The conversation had been more enjoyable when it revolved around DuskCabins.

"Do you think they're working?"

"Am I still rambling about curing all the world's diseases?" she replied lightly, though the memory of her psychosis made her stomach twist. The places that mania could take a person were not quite as light as her statement had made it out to be.

Her father laughed. "No, but what about the side effects?"

Tess frowned. That truly bothered her. The reduced physical energy from her medication had affected her ability to exercise, which in turn impacted how she perceived her body. She still hesitated to restart at the gym after her long stretch of inactivity during her hospital stay.

Then there was the medication's effect on her skin. While frustrating, it led her to learn more about makeup. It didn't feel so much like a necessity, but instead a tool to regain some control over her self-image. That was at least one positive outcome.

What weighed on her the most, though, was her concentration. She couldn't help but wonder if, without the meds, she might be even better at DuskCabins. Still, she was not willing to risk another manic episode just to find out.

"Manageable, " she said finally.

"I'm proud of you, kiddo."

She rolled her eyes at kiddo but gladly accepted the praise.

Their conversation turned to sports, which Tess only really followed to have something in common with her father. It was a welcome change from the heavier topics of her health, yet still different from the all-consuming DuskCabins.

As they neared the end of their neighborhood, they turned in an unspoken unison. Both were used to the same route they'd taken on every walk together.

Tess's phone buzzed. Glancing down, she felt a quick flash of disappointment when she saw that the text wasn't from Cade. That feeling quickly dissolved, though, as she read the message from her childhood best friend.

Andrea: I'm coming back next week. I hope we can catch up!

Andrea had visited Tess in the hospital, but Tess hadn't heard from her since. She was in an intensive engineering program at her school, so Tess didn't hold it against her. She typed out a response as she walked.

Tess: I'd love to! Is the semester over?
Andrea: Yes, it is! Jordan and Tara will be back, too, if you're feeling up to seeing them.

Tess frowned at the wording. She didn't like that Andrea still viewed her as someone who might not be up to seeing her own friends. Then again, Tess had to remind herself that the last place Andrea had seen her was in the hospital. Jordan, Tara, and Andrea had been her closest friends in high school, and they'd solidified their clique through countless sleepovers and late nights.

Tess: The four of us could get lunch at Gordon's. Wednesday at 1 pm?
Andrea: Sounds great! I'll let them know.

Tess grinned and slid her phone back into her pocket, but it buzzed again almost immediately.

"Someone's popular," her father joked. Then he pulled out his own phone and swiped his finger through notifications.

Tess rolled her eyes and then read the text.

Cade: ONE MORE DAY TO PRACTICE! Chippity chop!

Now Tess was beaming. Between the thought of reconnecting with her old friends and getting back to gaming with Cade, her day felt complete.

Tess: I'll be on in a sec. Finishing up a walk with my dad.
Cade: Ahh, tell him I say hi.
Tess: LOL no

Cade: Haha, why not? Parents usually love me.
Tess: fine.

As Tess and her father rounded the corner toward their driveway, she glanced at him, debating Cade's ridiculous request.

Still, she took a breath and said, "Dad...Cade says hi."

Her father stopped scrolling through his phone and looked at her, slightly amused.

"Tell him I say hi back and to win you some more money tonight."

Tess laughed at her father's blunt statement. "You know it's more me winning him the money."

"I see," her father replied as they approached the house, his tone skeptical.

Inside, Tess headed up the stairs and powered on her PC. As the machine hummed to life, she opened the game and noticed Cade already waiting for her in a party.

"He said hello and also asked for you to make me some money," Tess announced as soon as she joined.

Cade's deep laughter met her in return. "I'll make sure to earn you some money tonight."

"With my help, it seems possible," she remarked flatly. "How was your day?"

"It was fine." He never went into much detail there, but to be fair, neither did she.

"How was yours?" he asked.

"Fine as well. I spent a lot of time watching build fights on Twitch."

"As if you're not already outbuilding me every time already," Cade replied.

"True," Tess admitted with a grin, "but I could always learn how to outbuild you in a way that leaves you feeling even more defeated."

A new voice suddenly broke through the call. "Where's Snow White at?"

Tess's gaze darted to the profile. He wasn't one of her friends, so he had to be one of Cade's. Sometimes, old tournament opponents randomly joined their party, and Cade had to block them.

"Dan, you can't just join my party whenever you want," Cade said, his tone sharper than usual. "Tess and I are practicing for qualifiers."

Tess stiffened. Not only had Cade addressed this guy by his real name, but he had also casually confirmed his friend already knew who she was. That was new. She'd never met any of Cade's friends. He never even mentioned having any.

"The one and only Tess! I've heard so much about you. Wanna play with me some time and make me a quick hundo?"

Tess laughed lightly. She wouldn't mind playing with someone who was a friend of Cade's—perhaps she could learn something about his life outside the game. But before she could respond, Cade cut in with an unexpectedly harsh tone.

"She doesn't want to play with your sorry ass. Hit me up later, alright?"

"Alright, chill, dude. I was just wondering about our deal—"

"Hit me up later," he repeated, his voice even harsher.

It unsettled Tess; she'd never heard Cade speak that way.

"Alright, good luck. Nice to meet you, Tess." Dan sounded notably calmer than Cade.

"You too," Tess replied, her voice soft and uncertain.

With that, Dan left the party.

"Why does he call you Snow White?" Tess asked with a laugh, hoping to lighten the mood.

"It's a long story." Cade's response was short.

Sensing his unease, Tess turned the conversation back to the game. "I've been looking through the latest patch notes. We should review the best assault rifles to pick up before we start tonight."

Cade's demeanor changed as he responded, and their conversation returned to the game. In their first tournament, they placed second, winning $500 for the night. After that, they reinvested their winnings in some single-wager games, earning another $200. After the wagers, they cut themselves off. They needed to get ample sleep for their first qualifier attempt the next day

"The qualifier starts at one. How about we start practice around eleven in the morning?" Cade suggested as they wrapped up.

"Sounds good to me," Tess agreed.

They lingered in the lobby, sitting in comfortable silence. Sometimes, Tess wasn't ready to leave the comfort of their party, even if they were done playing. It seemed Cade often felt the same way. For Tess, these moments of quiet connection were invaluable. Sitting on the call with Cade, she felt less alone, even if neither of them said a word.

"My friends are returning from college next week," Tess said. She was not entirely sure why she told him; it had nothing to do with the game.

"That's great! Are you going to tell them about me?"

She laughed, relieved that he was responsive to the topic. "Of course. I can't wait to see what they think of my latest occupation."

"Are you still planning on returning to school?" he asked.

She paused. She wasn't entirely sure herself. "I guess it depends on what happens with the Grand Championship."

"Oh great. No pressure," he teased.

Tess laughed, knowing Cade thrived under pressure more than anyone she'd met.

"We could keep competing in new games as they come out," Cade suggested.

Tess considered it, but she wasn't sure how stable that plan would be for a long-term income. She hoped that an Esports team would be interested in hiring them as a duo—if they made it far enough in the competition.

"You could always go back to school, though," he added.

"I know," she replied. "I'll have to see what feels right when the time comes."

"Your friends might not understand that," he said. He sounded afraid. Maybe he was worried they would convince her to back out of the arrangement.

Tess hadn't really considered how they would react. She pondered it quietly for a moment. "I think they'll get it. They might even want to meet you," she said, considering Dan's earlier comment. She smirked, "...just like your buddy Dan wanted to meet me."

Cade's tone shifted. "Dan is not my buddy."

"Oh, I'm sorry...he seemed nice enough."

"It's alright. I better get some sleep for tomorrow, Tess. Goodnight."

The abruptness stung.

"Goodnight," she replied quietly.

Cade left the party, and Tess sat alone at her PC, staring at her small friends list. There wasn't a single person on it that she wouldn't want to introduce to Cade. It felt like he was embarrassed by her. Shaking off the hurt, she scrolled through game updates and details about tomorrow's tournament, trying to focus. With how much was at stake, there was no room for hurt feelings.

Tomorrow would be their first shot. She logged off, took her pills, and fell asleep quickly, her mind already anticipating the battles ahead.

Chapter Eight
Taking a Shot

Tess and Cade sat silently in the DuskCabins lobby, with their first qualifier match looming. They would play three games, and their final kill count from each would be added together and compared to all other people playing in qualification mode. Winning the match entirely provided a three-point bonus.

Tess broke the silence. "You know my thing with breathing and playing at the same time…it's just—"

"Tess, you know how to breathe," Cade reassured her. "This is just another tournament. It's not any different from the others we've played. You're going to do great."

Tess exhaled sharply, shaking her head. How was Cade always so calm? He made mistakes, too, but somehow, he didn't get stuck on them. Meanwhile, she was haunted by every error, every wrong move, every hesitation.

"Tess, I know you're still freaking out over there…I told you; you'll be great."

Her fingers drummed on her desk. "You don't know everything, Cade." Her response wasn't as light as intended. The stress was really getting to her.

"Woah, Miss Attitude. They call me Cade 'the All-Knowing', haven't you heard?"

"Who are they?" she laughed.

"You know…people."

"They seem to be pretty dumb," she teased.

It sounded like Cade was about to retort, but a warning flashed on the screen, silencing them both. The first match would begin in ten seconds.

"Just like every other tournament," she reminded herself. Taking a deep breath, she recalled the countless victories they had under their belt and let a slight smile tug at her lips. This would be no different.

They dropped into the jungle on the outskirts of the map and stocked up on supplies. There, they ran into one duo. They left at full health with two kills. After that, they pushed into the center of the map, taking down two more teams on their way. By the time the zone closed in on Metropolis with twelve players remaining, they had a total kill score of six.

"You good on shotty ammo?" Cade called from the top of a stone tower on the edge of Metropolis, clearing the rooms of what few supplies remained.

"All set there. Do you have any AR?" Tess asked, keeping watch from the bottom floor. Her eyes scanned the city from the front window, looking for any sign of movement.

"I'll bring some down."

As Cade spoke, Tess spotted two teams exchanging fire on the right side of the city. Her grip tightened on her rifle. It was a perfect opportunity, but it would be risky to intervene. Six other players were undoubtedly hiding, biding their time, and watching as well.

Cade approached from behind moments later, dropping fifty assault rifle rounds into Tess's hands.

"They're going to get third partied," he said, noticing the same battle.

"I know, but I think we should at least get a move on finding the other teams that are hiding. Six kills will not secure us a spot at the top."

Cade nodded thoughtfully and scanned the town again. "Let's push through the outskirts and flush out the stragglers."

He darted out the back door, and Tess followed closely behind. They stalked through three different shops before stopping in their tracks. As Cade had predicted, the two fighting teams had been cleared out by a third team perched in a sniper's tower. The same sniper tower that Tess and Cade now stood next to.

They crouched behind a dumpster in the neighboring alley. If the snipers were to notice them from above, it would do little to provide protection. Luckily, the players remained fixated on the city's center, oblivious to Tess and Cade creeping up from behind.

"If we move through the base of the tower and up to the roof, they'll hear us coming," Cade said, his tone cautious.

Tess agreed, but they weren't left with many other choices. If they attempted to build up to the roof, it would also be noisy, and with the angle they had now—staring up at the top of the tower from the ground—it would not be an easy fight.

"I'll build up alone. Once they turn on me, cover me," Tess said, her voice steady.

"Alright."

If Cade agreed, Tess knew it had to be the best move strategically. She waved her hand, forming ramps that circled the tower, and headed straight for the roof. As she predicted, the snipers turned on her, but they still hadn't noticed Cade.

As the players tucked away their sniper rifles and pulled out shotguns, Cade unloaded assault rifle shots. His shots landed hard, forcing the enemies to scramble for cover. Tess closed in as Cade continued to unload on the players, tearing down their walls and allowing Tess the opportunity to get in a few shotgun shots. After connecting some, both the players were killed. The tower was theirs.

Tess quickly boxed herself in with walls for cover and rifled through the loot scattered across the roof. There were now four players left in the game, and they were probably very aware of Tess and Cade's locations due to the gunfire. They would need to regroup. A notification appeared at the top of Tess's screen.

BlackLantern has been knocked.

"Fuck, a sniper got me!" Cade shouted.

"Get behind the trashcans again! I'm coming," Tess responded.

Since he'd been shot by a long-range weapon, the player had to be far. With luck, she'd have enough time to revive him. Instead of risking exposure with her ramps on the exterior of the building, Tess moved inside through the different floors, which provided better cover. When she reached the bottom, she shoved open the back door and dragged Cade's downed body inside.

"Hold still," she muttered, hurriedly wrapping his arms with bandages.

"There's four left," he said hastily. The circle was getting tighter, and all the duos would have no choice but to face each other soon. "We're at eight points. I think that's pretty decent."

Tess taped off the last bandage, and he stood back up.

"I agree. We should lay low and aim for the bonus points," Tess replied.

Outside, shotgun shots echoed through the street; at least two of the teams had started fighting.

"Unless we could safely third party," Cade suggested. He rolled his injured arm back and forth, seeming to test it.

"Let's head back to the roof. The players we killed left two gold sniper rifles behind," Tess said as she began sprinting back up the stairs.

They collected the golden sniper rifles on the roof and quickly constructed a small fort for cover. They peered over the walls, looking for the other fighters, but all they could make out were empty roads.

Gunfire sounded from the left.

"More shots," Tess muttered, her head snapping toward the sound. "They must be inside a building somewhere."

"I think they're in the market building," Cade responded.

A notification flashed at the top of the screen.

TiredAgent23
eliminated.

Now, it was just Tess, Cade, and the final duo.

Tess exhaled and aimed her sniper rifle at the market building's entrance. Moments later, the last two players walked straight into the open. She didn't hesitate. Her shot rang out, but the duo was ready. They dodged left and quickly constructed walls around themselves.

"They're good," she sighed.

"Now they know we're here," Cade said, a slight edge to his voice.

Tess glanced at him, frowning. "I think the giant forts on the roof of the sniper tower were already a dead giveaway."

The two players set up their own fort system on the street below Tess and Cade's tower, their walls climbing higher with each passing second. A sniper shot rang past Tess's left ear.

She narrowed her eyes. Tess preferred close combat and build battles, where she could take control of the terrain, as opposed to this long-distance chicken game, but she knew she'd receive a lecture from Cade if she were to drop down from their high ground.

She stood up and pulled out her assault rifle, spraying rapidly at the forts on the ground. Cade continued to take calculated and paced shots with his sniper rifle.

Their focus was split—Tess keeping the pressure on with rapid-fire while Cade continued more precise shots with the sniper rifle. The battle heated up, and the circle would force them closer any second.

"I'd be better if I dropped down," Tess complained.

"We have the height advantage. Let's wait." Cade's steady voice did little to soothe her impatience.

Before she could argue, Tess was pierced in the heart by a bullet. She dropped to the ground and was stuck, motionless, next to Cade. The other team wasted no time. Encouraged by their knock, they began building rapidly toward the roof. Cade hesitated for a moment, glancing between Tess and the approaching players.

"There's no time to revive me," Tess said. "Just try to get the kills."

Cade nodded, refocusing on the fight. He scrambled to maintain the height advantage, building upward as fast as possible, but the opposing duo closed in from both sides. He didn't stand a chance.

VICTORY: EFN Perktuns and EFN Nautalus

Tess's jaw dropped. They had been playing against EFN Perktuns. The competition really was stiff.

"Don't tell me you're fan-girling during our loss," Cade muttered, unimpressed.

Her jaw closed, and she frowned, thinking about losing those three victory points. They returned to the lobby, and a five-minute timer displayed in the corner. When it was complete, their next match would begin.

While playing their game with only one hundred other players in their lobby, thousands of other games took place worldwide, and a scoreboard was posted with the results of every duo's scores.

With a score of eight, they were 1,007 out of 53,600. The top one hundred started at a score of fifteen and went up to twenty-three. It was dominated by professional Esports players. Tess leaned back in her chair, arms crossed. A score of eight would get them a lot further in a simple wager tournament, but these qualifiers seemed like they'd be different.

"We're better than 52,000 people, Tess!" Cade said, trying to lift her spirits.

"We're not aggressive enough," she replied, shaking her head.

Cade's preference for careful strategy had worked before, but it wasn't cutting it against their competition's aggressive playstyle.

"You're right," Cade admitted after a moment. "I didn't realize how high the others' scores would be. It might be too hard to catch up in just two games. At least we know now. And at least we'll get twenty of the best teams out of the way for next week."

Tess felt a pang of disappointment at his words. She'd wanted him to say they still had a shot this week, even if it wasn't true. But deep down, she knew he was right.

They played out the next two games more aggressively and ended the first with a score of 12, then the second with a quick loss, only scoring 4. In the end, they stood at 8,023 of the 53,600 competitors. Their last game set them back quite a bit.

EFN Perktuns qualified along with his teammate and eighteen others. After all the matches were over, Cade was silent on the other end of the call. The last game brought down his spirit.

"We're still going to make it!" Tess surprised herself when she said it. Usually, Cade gave the pep talks, but she could tell the last game had left him really disappointed.

"We're going to need a lot more practice," he responded, his tone more muted than ever before.

"If we focus on aggressive gameplay and practice building this week, I know we can get further next week." Tess kept her voice firm.

She believed in the progress they'd made and their ability to improve. She liked having something to believe in. Something that was in her control. She needed this tournament more than he knew.

"Hey, Cade, you did great today, by the way."

"Didn't know you went and became a cheerleader on me."

She could still hear the sad tone underneath the careful humor, but she smirked, nonetheless.

"Don't get used to it."

Chapter Nine
Opening the Floodgates

The next few days flew by as Tess and Cade entered their very own DuskCabins boot camp. They pushed each other to the limit, churning out tournaments more rapidly than ever before.

At times, Cade grew frustrated with the aggressive strategy, but he was slowly adjusting. Tess, on the other hand, was thriving. Still, Cade often had to remind her to slow down. Her reckless speed led to a quick death more than once.

Before Tess knew it, Tuesday arrived. The day she would be meeting her new therapist. Although it was nice to be sucked into the DuskCabins world so heavily, she was glad to finally be doing something else.

She warned Cade that she would be out in the morning, meaning he would have to train alone, but she didn't explain why. He didn't press her for details either, which was a relief. She appreciated that he never pried into her personal life, and she returned the favor.

Tess still didn't know what Cade did when he was not playing DuskCabins. He wasn't a very open person, but she felt comfortable with him and trusted him. She figured they would learn more about each other in time, but when it came to her mental health, she was alright with that time being postponed.

Tess walked into the waiting room in her outpatient mental health facility and met the secretary's smile with one of her own. The secretary was familiarly excitable as she handed Tess a brown clipboard stacked with paperwork. Her sleeve inched up, and a lotus tattoo peeked through.

"Hey, girl, here's what you need to fill out for your first one-on-one. I'll let Amber know you're here."

Amber. Tess had already forgotten the woman's name. She was expected to spill her entire guts to this woman and couldn't even remember her name. Tess took the clipboard and sat down in one of the waiting room chairs. She put the pen to the top of the paper and began to work through the survey.

In the past week, how many times have you believed that you have supernatural abilities?

Tess winced and scribbled down a 0. She knew why the question was there. It was something she had believed while manic. She made her way through the rest of the survey, then sat and stared across at the empty pale blue wall, pencil tapping on the clipboard.

"Tess?" a careful yet warm voice called a few minutes later.

Tess looked up from her finished paperwork and saw a woman, probably just a few years older than her, waiting at the open door. Her outfit was trendy. She looked like someone Tess could be friends with, which was not exactly what Tess had experienced before in her therapy.

"I'm Amber." She extended her hand, and Tess stood to shake it. Up close, Tess noticed faint wrinkles.

"You can follow me back," Amber said.

As they passed the group room, Tess peered inside. She realized that she no longer recognized any of the faces—apart from Melinda's—who leaned in toward a young woman at the center of the room.

"You were in Melinda's group, right?" Amber asked.

"Yeah..." Tess said.

She wondered if Melinda had said anything negative about her to Amber. Would Amber judge her for resenting the treatment?

Amber led Tess into a small office dominated by shades of cyan blue. A small couch sat near a desk, an antique wooden table held a decorative crystal, and a shelf was stocked with an array of psychology books.

Tess instinctively sat on the couch, and Amber sat across from her at the desk. She set the paperwork to her right and focused on Tess instead, which surprised Tess. As far as she'd experienced, paperwork seemed to be a therapist's priority, usually over the act of therapy itself.

"How was the group for you?"

Tess looked at her hands, which were nervously grabbing at the edges of the couch cushion. She felt like she was under a microscope, afraid Amber would not like her so much if she admitted how she slacked off in Melinda's group.

"It was alright," she said quietly.

"Depending on your situation and openness, I know that group can be beneficial...or sometimes not." Her tone was empathetic, not harsh, and Tess glanced up to meet her gaze.

"I felt like my problems were kind of disconnected from the other people. Not in an egotistical way. I mean, I'm sure their issues were pressing to them..." Her voice trailed off as she gazed out the window, and she scrambled through her thoughts, searching for a better way to explain it.

"That is completely okay, Tess. Just because someone has a valid issue, it does not mean that we all inherently relate to it. Sometimes it works out that way in groups, but sometimes it does not."

Was this woman a mind reader? Or perhaps Melinda had said something to her. Her chest sunk. If they were talking about her behind her back, it was a problem. She didn't trust that Melinda fully understood her, so now Amber may not either.

"Did Melinda say something about me?"

Amber's eyebrows arched briefly but quickly returned to a neutral expression. "We don't talk to each other about our patients. The only time we may reach out to someone is if you or someone else is in danger."

Tess untensed at the explanation. She'd heard it many times before, but she hadn't applied it to the current situation. Amber leaned forward, her desk chair squeaking slightly with the shift in weight.

"Now, I want you to tell me a little bit about yourself. What brought you here?" she asked.

"I answered some of that on the survey." Tess gestured to the table.

"I know you did," Amber patted the paperwork, "...but I'd like to hear it from you."

Tess took a deep breath and leaned back. She closed her eyes and focused on the white noise machine that hummed outside the door.

"Well...I've been in a lot of therapy for depression and anxiety since I was a kid. I don't think I've ever really participated correctly, but I've made it through life alright...until this first semester at college. I partied, and drank, but I still kept up with my academic work. I was under more pressure and stress than ever before, and one day I just started not making sense anymore."

Tess's voice caught for a moment, and she cleared her throat.

"It got worse from there; I couldn't sleep; I had so many racing thoughts—so many theories? I started to drive my friends away. My parents took me to the hospital, and that's where I really lost it. I blacked out for almost a week until one day...I just snapped out of it."

"After that, they told me I had Bipolar Disorder I, and what I experienced was a textbook manic episode with psychosis. They put me on new medications and shipped me out into group therapy. I ended up withdrawing from the semester."

She exhaled as she finished recounting her experience. She realized she'd been speaking quickly, her gaze fixed on the cars rushing outside past the window. She hadn't cried, which she was proud of. When she met Amber's gaze again, the therapist nodded sympathetically.

Amber asked, "What do you mean, Tess, when you say you haven't participated in therapy correctly?"

Tess blinked in surprise. She expected Amber to dig into the theories and the blackout, not to focus on this part of the story.

"Well, I mean—and I said this in the group as well—I feel like if you go to therapy but aren't willing to talk about what's really bothering you, you can't expect to make much progress."

"That's a good point. Have you felt that way about yourself before?"

"Yes. I think earlier, when I was in therapy, I was unwilling to open up. I know that's the point of therapy, but it's sometimes a difficult thing for me...to be vulnerable."

"Well, you're doing an excellent job of being open right now. It's also very common to feel uncomfortable when you are vulnerable."

Amber's nose scrunched up as she smiled warmly. Tess returned the gesture genuinely.

"Do you mind telling me a little more about what happened leading up to your hospitalization?" Amber asked.

Tess's smile faltered. Recalling this episode was what she'd been avoiding so carefully for so long.

"It started off one random Monday night. I was up late, jotting down creative writing ideas in my notes app. I didn't sleep that entire night. My ideas turned into theories about the world, and they didn't stop coming. All through my classes, I couldn't focus. I began to share the theories with anyone who would listen.

"I am not typically outgoing. Everyone was surprised to hear me say so much. I thought I could cure all diseases. I thought I could become a God. Looking back, I know I sounded insane, but in the moment, I thought I was some kind of genius."

Now, tears welled in Tess's eyes, burning as they streamed down her cheeks. She blinked and tensed in anticipation of the classic giving of tissues that would occur to passively acknowledge her tears, but instead, Amber pressed on like normal.

"And how did things change at the hospital?"

Tess gripped the couch cushion.

"At the hospital, the delusions just really came in at full force. I thought the hospital was an escape room at first. Later, I thought the nurses were trying to kill me. It felt like I was about to die over and over again in so many different ways...it still haunts me now. I know now that it wasn't real, so it shouldn't weigh on me like something that actually happened, but it still does."

The tears fell faster, and Tess winced. When she closed her eyes, all she saw were the white hospital walls. All she felt was that urgency, that certainty that she was about to die.

"It sounds like you were trapped in fight-or-flight mode the whole time. That is a very stressful state of being. It makes perfect sense that the trauma still weighs on you. Even if those beliefs were not grounded in reality, you still went through all the emotions as if they were."

Amber paused until Tess nodded along in agreement.

"Those are experiences we can safely work through here, too, but we don't have to press on them right now. Instead, I want to talk about your diagnosis. How did it make you feel, receiving it?"

Tess breathed out and forced the manic memories away. She grabbed the box of tissues on the table and took one out to wipe her face. "I felt kind of defeated. They told me I would have to treat this for the rest of my life. I don't like the medication side effects."

"Do you like your psychiatrist?"

"She's good." Tess had an understanding psychiatrist, but there were still going to be side effects with whatever medicine she took.

"Perhaps bring up the issues you're having with the side effects." Amber paused to scribble down a note, then she continued, "Before you were diagnosed, what did your mental health treatment look like? You said you had experience with therapy?"

Tess nodded.

"Yeah, I was in therapy all through high school. I guess mental health is something I've been treating my whole life. It just didn't feel so permanent until now."

"That makes sense. Try to think of this as a continuation of that treatment you've been doing all along."

"Another thing that I felt with the diagnosis..." Tess paused. Was she really going to open up about all of this? Every word felt like a weight lifting off her chest, so she decided to keep going. "I felt numb. Like...I expected everything to either get better or worse, but they were just words in the end. They didn't change who I was, where I was, or anything really."

"I think that's a valuable realization, Tess. In your position, a lot of people feel like they are defined by their diagnosis, but as you said, it does not change who you were before. They're simply words that help professionals and you seek the resources you need to succeed."

Tess smiled. She was glad she shared that thought in the end. It felt like the session was ending so quickly. They went through the paperwork and scheduled another meeting for the same time next Tuesday. Tess left the building feeling the same lightness she did after a successful DuskCabins tournament. And as she thought about playing again, that lightness only grew.

Chapter Ten
Flooding

Saturday morning, Tess and Cade sat in the DuskCabins practice mode preparing for their second shot at qualifiers. Since Tuesday, Cade had made continuous progress in aggressive gameplay, while Tess worked on exercising restraint. Still, since Tuesday, they'd lost more tournaments than they'd won, and that was because Tess was distracted.

It had started with Tuesday's therapy session. Though effective, it had pried open a floodgate of memories she'd perfectly stored away. Now, she couldn't walk halfway through Metropolis without triggering a flashback to her manic episode.

"I don't understand what changed."

Tess winced at the statement, but Cade's tone wasn't laced with anger. He simply sounded confused. They'd played two warm-up games. Both ended quickly with low kill counts, and the morale for qualifiers was quickly depleting.

"I just...I haven't felt like myself recently," Tess said, staring down at her fuzzy pink socks as she readjusted her headset.

"You said that yesterday. But we're back in the qualifiers today. Tess, this is beyond feeling like yourself. You need to put that other stuff aside—at least while we're competing."

"I know," Tess agreed. "I just...I can't explain it, alright? It's personal."

"Personal?" Cade said with a sharper tone. It was the first time Tess heard him sound truly angry. "We only have three more chances to qualify. You need to get over whatever this is."

"I'm trying, Cade. Sometimes the shit I deal with can't just be relieved by your attempts to tease the anxiety out of me. Why should I tell you anything anyway?" She shrank into the back of her gaming chair. "I know nothing about your life, your job, or what you do for fun. All we talk about is DuskCabins, and we keep it that way for a reason. This is business, Cade."

Tears streamed down her face, but he'd never know; her voice didn't waver. She wiped her eyes with her sleeve and silently cursed herself for the constant waterworks.

"Alright," Cade said after a moment, his voice softened. "I'm sorry, Tess. I won't push you on it anymore. I'm just nervous."

"I know," Tess replied. "Me too. I'm gonna make changes."

She was going to have to try harder to shove her memories back wherever they were hiding before her individual therapy began. She imagined putting all those moments into a box and then stuffing that box way back into her brain. Then, she imagined locking that box and closing it inside multiple vaults for good measure.

"Let's try facing each other with the shotguns again," she said after a moment.

"Sure, and I have something for you," Cade said.

"What's that?" Tess looked at her phone, anticipating a forgotten Venmo payment from one of their wager games.

"Turn around."

Tess's eyes widened and she turned to face the back of her bedroom as if he'd be standing there waiting. Nothing was out of place.

"Did you just turn around in real life?" Cade started laughing.

"Maybe…" Tess turned a shade of pink while she returned her gaze to the computer. Inside the DuskCabins practice island, she turned around.

Cade stood behind her with a collection of wildflowers.

"I thought they'd make you feel better," he said.

In reality, these were meaningless pixels he must have gathered from the bushes while they were talking, but they sent her heart racing for some reason. Tess reached out her arms, and Cade dropped the flowers into her inventory.

"Thanks," she managed.

"Cost me a fortune," Cade said casually.

Tess rolled her eyes.

The rest of the morning was filled with better games. They broke for lunch, and before she knew it, they were dropping into their first qualifier game. With their new aggressive strategy applied, their first game ended with a score of eighteen—landing them at 33 of 51,200 competitors.

Their second was even stronger. They scored twenty-one, pushing their rank to 12th overall.

"This is insane," Tess breathed.

"We've got this," Cade replied, and the warmth in his voice made something soften in her chest.

They stood shoulder to shoulder inside the plane, and the DuskCabins island quickly came into view. It was a patchwork of green hills, cities, and compounds sitting in the middle of a violet sea. After a few moments, they dove out the side and headed straight for Metropolis.

Peeking past her whipping hair, Tess made out dozens of other duos aiming for the city. Her hands clenched into fists.

They landed in the southwest corner of Metropolis, choosing a discreet coffee shop unlikely to be looted immediately. Cade took the lead and broke through the pitched roof, dropping into the attic. It served as a storage room for the shop.

Tess followed closely behind, running past him and sweeping the downstairs area. She grabbed an assault rifle near the espresso machine, a sniper rifle from underneath a table, and some armor that was lying on the counter.

"You see a shotty?" she called up to Cade.

"Nope," he replied from above.

She sighed. She needed a shotgun for their new playstyle to work. Slipping out the front of the café, she headed to the building next door. It was a steel tower with a large glass entrance. She paused just outside, listening for footsteps. There was no movement inside, so she pushed through the glass doors. The interior was drab. The walls were painted plain white, and stretchers lined the hallway. Slowly, Tess realized this was a hospital.

"Where'd you go?" Cade's voice sounded over a walkie-talkie in her pack.

Though his volume remained constant no matter how far she was in the game, it felt more distant from this room. She was entranced by the plain white walls and how familiar they felt.

The hospital in her memory came rushing back. The way they suffocated her. The way no one listened to her when she tried to explain their evil plans. No one would hear her out. Why would they hear her out? She wasn't making any sense. And yet she knew, she felt, the walls they were trying to kill her.

A shotgun rang out.

She gasped. The walls had killed her. She was right.

"Tess!"

No. She was wrong. She was in DuskCabins, and she'd been shot down. She stared up at an astronaut who quickly finished her off, preventing any chance of revival.

"Tess, what the fuck just happened?"

"I went to look for a shotty," she whispered.

Cade wasn't trying to hide his anger, and he had every right to be angry. She'd just thrown away their best shot yet.

"I'm sorry...I'm so sorry." Her voice broke this time, revealing the tears that were likely to return.

"It's alright, Tess," he said. "I'm still alive… it's alright."

How could it be alright when she ruined their chance to qualify? They had been so close. Tess watched silently as Cade reverted to his careful strategy for the rest of the match.

He managed to get five kills before being brought down by a duo that was far too coordinated for him to fight alone. When they backed out of the game, the leaderboard showed them at 50th place. That number would drop even lower once the rest of the matches wrapped up.

"We're not going to the Grand Championship," Tess stated in defeat.

"We still have two more shots, Tess. We're going to make it!"

Not if she couldn't get her memories under control. Ever since she'd opened up in therapy, everything had started flooding back faster, louder, and more often. But day by day, the surge was slowing. They'd pulled off two high-kill games before the slip. She just needed that time between tides to keep expanding.

"Look who's the cheerleader now," she teased, though her voice still held the weight of disappointment.

He laughed, but she could hear it in him too.

"I'm going to get myself sorted out before next weekend," she said. "That will be our weekend." She wasn't sure if she was trying to convince him or herself.

"And we're sticking with the aggressive strategy," he added. "I still need the practice."

"You did great today."

"So did you...up until that last slip-up..." He cleared his throat. "...but hey, mistakes happen to all of us. All we can do is work toward next weekend. Your friends are coming this week, right?"

Tess perked up. She'd nearly forgotten. "You're right! That's gonna be great. I can't wait to see what they think of all this video game stuff."

"Let's take a break and then do some wager games later tonight."

"Sounds good."

Tess logged off her PC, let out a long sigh, and headed down to the kitchen. Outside the backdoor, she saw her brother sprinting around the yard with some of his friends. Her parents stood at the counter, making sandwiches.

"How'd it go?" her father asked.

"We lost," Tess said simply.

Her mother looked up at Tess with sympathy. "I'm sorry, Tess. Just think how far you've come with this game, even if you don't qualify."

"We're still going to qualify," Tess snapped back.

"You've got two more chances," her father added hurriedly, trying to lighten the mood.

Still, her mother's expression remained apprehensive. Tess could tell she was already bracing for the worst.

"I'm not going back to therapy," Tess announced as she walked casually toward the fridge and grabbed an apple.

Her mother dropped a butter knife, and her father's eyes shot up from where he was rustling through a turkey bag.

"Uh, yes, you are," her mother replied.

"I'm not ready for it," Tess insisted.

"If you live in this house, we expect you to take the best care of your health. That means attending therapy," her father said.

"I have a check for you." Tess pulled an envelope from her back pocket and placed it on the counter.

Her parents exchanged a puzzled expression.

"It's the cost of my hospitalization. I'm making enough money from the game to cover my health expenses. And I'm telling you, what is best for me right now is taking a break from therapy. I'm an adult. You can't force me to go."

Her father opened the envelope and studied the check. Her mother stepped closer to look, then glanced back at Tess, unsure.

It was true that Tess was an adult. She was no longer required to go to therapy as she had finished her mandatory outpatient group. Tess knew her parents would never kick her out, and she figured now was the best time to present them with the money.

"You are an adult, Tess, but I expect you to make better choices for your health. We appreciate the money, but I'm worried about how much you're gaming. It seems very intense."

"Well," Tess said, biting her apple, "you can keep worrying. That's out of my control. I've made up my mind."

She turned and started walking out of the kitchen.

"Oh—Dad, do you want to go on our walk at three today?"

He blinked, caught off guard. "I guess…"

Tess quickly returned up the stairs and dropped into solo games until Cade returned.

Chapter Eleven
An Engineer, Politician, Artist, and Dropout Walk into a Restaurant

Day by day, Tess's gameplay was getting better. Quitting therapy, just as she had started to make real progress, felt wrong. But the tournament was the biggest opportunity of her life thus far, and she wanted to give it everything.

Other than the weight of that decision, Tess felt comfortable with how her life was going. The steady income with Cade continued, and as their gameplay synced up again, things became better between them. In fact, with the aggressive playstyle, they were better than ever, and Tess felt increasingly disconnected from the real world as she sunk into their games.

That's why the thought of seeing Andrea and her other friends for the first time in a while stirred up some anxiety when Wednesday came around. Sometimes, it was more comfortable hiding out in DuskCabins world. Tess felt safe there.

"Tessa!" That anxious feeling faded when Andrea's warm, familiar voice cut through Gordon's parking lot.

Tess stepped out of her car and saw Andrea standing across the asphalt lot.

'Tessa' was a nickname Andrea had coined in high school the first time they sat together in class. She had simply mispronounced her name, but it stuck as a joke between the two of them to this day.

Andrea turned to make a direct path to her, and Tess braced herself for the collision of their bodies in one of Andrea's caring yet tight hugs. Andrea squeezed Tess into a firm embrace, and Tess rested her head on her shoulder and closed her eyes. The familiar feeling made her heart feel heavy, and her eyes watered.

"I missed you," Tess murmured.

She hadn't realized how much so until this moment either.

"I missed you too." Andrea let go and grinned.

Tess admired Andrea's trendy outfit, neat orange braids, and flawless, freckled face. She'd never seen Andrea wear makeup, and she didn't need it.

"Look at you! There's life in those eyes."

Tess laughed. She must have set a low standard the last time they had seen each other. That had been right after she snapped out of the mania. That had been possibly the lowest point of her life and a much more sedated one in terms of medication.

"I've felt more alive lately..." she said eventually.

A car whooshed past them on the main road bordering the diner.

"I'm so happy to see you like this, and that smokey eye is killer."

Tess had passed on her usual t-shirt and sweatpants combo, going for a trendier look instead—something she might have worn back when she was attending college classes every day. She'd even invested time in her makeup, putting to use all the hours she'd poured into tutorials on YouTube.

"Thank you!" Tess replied, a small smile forming.

Andrea glanced toward a buzzing phone in her hands, then back to Tess.

"Jordan texted our group. She and Tara are already inside. We better go meet them."

Tess felt a flicker of disappointment. They were in a group chat without her. But she reasoned with herself—this was bound to happen since they attended the same college without her.

She followed Andrea into the restaurant. A bell chimed as she pushed through a glass door, revealing an empty wooden host stand. Tess peered toward the back at their favorite booth on the far left. Jordan and Tara were already seated there, waving.

Andrea, who must have noticed them too, started across the diner. Tess followed, weaving through a few wooden tables. As they walked, she glanced at the wall. One of Tara's paintings from high school was still up for sale. An intricate arrangement of flowers. It hung with a mix of other local art pieces. Tess smiled softly, then looked back at her friends, the grin widening.

Jordan was Vietnamese with a strong athletic build. She currently wore a Dungeons and Dragons T-shirt with cargo pants. Across from her sat Tara, who had almond skin and beautiful thick black hair. She was wearing a long, flowing summer dress. It might've looked out of place in such a casual atmosphere on anyone else, but when Tara wore it, it seemed like the dress belonged nowhere else.

They both stood to hug Tess and then the four sat to fill the booth. Pop music played softly in the distance, blending with the murmur of other groups chatting inside the diner.

"How was your semester?" Tess asked. It felt like a simple enough opener, and she also genuinely wanted to know how it had panned out for all of them. Andrea was studying engineering, Jordan political science, and Tara fine arts.

"It went by in a blur," Jordan spoke first.

"For me, it was more like never-ending critiques. Not so blurry," Tara added with a wince.

"Never-ending stress," Andrea finished, shaking her head.

Tess nodded with a smile.

"I think you made the right choice by getting out of the whole thing," Jordan joked.

Andrea shot her a quick look, and Jordan seemed to instantly regret the words—but Tess just laughed.

The girls went into more detail about their specific programs until the waiter arrived, balancing four glasses of water on a tray. He passed them around the table and then took their orders.

"So, what have you been up to?" Tara asked.

Jordan and Andrea nodded and looked at her with intrigue.

"I was in a group for a while, but now I'm done with therapy," Tess said.

Andrea looked confused. "Done? That was fast..."

Tess reconsidered her statement. "Done for the time being, at least. It was just starting to bring up a lot of bad memories."

Jordan glanced at Tara, but Tess couldn't tell what they were thinking. Tess considered expanding on it, but she was sick of explaining herself. "Something else has been taking up most of my time."

Andrea's face brightened. "Oh yeah, what would that be?"

"I've been making thousands of dollars playing DuskCabins."

Andrea and Jordan started laughing, and Tara choked on her water.

Once Tara's throat cleared, she squealed, "You became an E-girl streamer while we were gone?"

Now Tess was laughing, but Tara's concerned expression didn't fade.

"No. I've been competing off-stream—in tournaments."

"Wait, you're not kidding?" Andrea asked.

"Nope," Tess replied. "I paid off my medical bills, and now I'm aiming to pay off my student debt."

"That's crazy! All I know about that game is my little brother plays it more than he goes outside. He hasn't made any money, though," Jordan said.

"Yeah, it's not about money for everyone, but I've been competing in tournaments with this guy I met online. We're both really good, and we're trying to get into the Grand Championship."

"The what-now?" Tara asked.

"It's this huge competition for the game with millions up to win. Only the best of the best get in, and a lot of the people that have already qualified are professional gamers."

"Do you think you have a shot?" Jordan asked.

"It sounds like our Tessa does. Geez, thousands of dollars!" Andrea's expression shifted into a smirk. "What I want to know is: who's this guy you're playing with?"

Tess couldn't help the grin that spread across her face at the thought of Cade. Her finger traced a hole in the booth's cushion as she thought carefully about how to explain him to her friends.

"He found me somehow based on my in-game statistics and this website for streaming video games called Twitch. We clicked instantly as a duo, and he's just...he's great."

"How old is he?" Tara furrowed her brow.

"Twenty-one."

"Is he in college? What does he do? Just play games?" Jordan jumped in.

Tess frowned. She was not prepared for a full-on interrogation about Cade, partly because she didn't have the answers herself. It was starting to frustrate her more and more, but at the same time, they had a whole world to talk about in the game, so it made sense that outside things just didn't come up.

"His work is flexible."

Jordan and Tara sat back in their seats, seeming to note Tess's frustration.

Andrea picked the conversation back up. "Well, is he cute or what? Do you have pictures? Instagram?"

Tess smiled again. She knew this would be Andrea's concern.

"He doesn't use Instagram, but I can show you his Venmo picture. I think he's cute."

Andrea laughed. "This really is a business relationship."

"Well, it's more than that, at least," Tess said, feeling a little defensive as she swiped through her phone to find Venmo.

"Does that mean our Tessa is finally in love?" Tara teased.

Tess laughed, but her cheeks warmed as blood rushed to her face. "Okay, I wouldn't go that far."

"How could she love him, Tara? She hasn't met him in real life," Jordan said like it was a simple math equation.

"Exactly," Tess agreed, but some part of her wasn't certain. She was starting to question whether you had to meet someone in person to develop feelings for them.

Finally, she found his photo. She slid her phone across the table for the others to see. They all seemed to agree with her judgment.

A few moments later, their food arrived. The waiter placed a warm chicken and avocado melt on the table before Tess. The smell of the cheddar cheese was intoxicating.

"Does he seem trustworthy?" Andrea asked. It was the first serious question she had asked all day.

Tess considered it for a moment. Cade had always paid her fairly for the tournaments. He seemed to understand her, never spoke to her poorly. Sure, there was more to his story, but that was the case with anyone really.

"He does," Tess answered.

"Well, then, I'm so excited for you!" Andrea said. Her words were passionate, and her eyes light.

"Remember us when you are video game famous," Jordan joked before biting into her veggie burger.

"God, we missed you," Tara said softly.

Tess smiled. She had missed this, too. She hadn't been able to talk about Cade with anyone her age, and she was tired of hearing what her parents had to say.

The rest of the meal slipped by with laughter and memories. Once, in high school, the four of them had been grouped together for a biology project. It ended up being a real test of their friendship.

Tara admitted that she had not understood any material from the unit. Tess defended her participation as the group's secretary. Andrea didn't say much, but they all remembered she was the backbone of that project.

They also talked about their plans for the upcoming summer. Andrea already had an internship lined up, Tara was working at an art shop in their hometown, and Jordan was still waiting to hear back from different opportunities. The conversation wavered back to Tess and video games, but the others had a limited understanding of the topic, so it couldn't go too far.

By the end of lunch, Tess felt like a new person. She had almost forgotten what it was like to be around her friends in person, and now, after being with them, she felt so much relief about her life in general.

They paid the bill and headed out, with Tess promising to update them on her tournament progress through a new group text. For once, when she arrived home, Tess didn't jump right on her computer.

Chapter Twelve
Third Time's a Charm

"You've been on fire lately," Cade exclaimed. They'd just won another match with a high kill score of eighteen. It was Saturday morning, and their third shot at the qualifier's tournament quickly approached.

Since Wednesday, Tess had felt a newfound energy. For the first time, her friends were checking in on her progress and cheering her on. It was an added motivation.

"You haven't been so bad yourself," Tess replied. She couldn't take a compliment or apparently return one.

"So bad? Uh, have you seen my outplays recently?" He didn't seem fazed by her lack of affection.

"Alright, alright, you're on fire too," she caved in with a grin.

They had half an hour left before the tournament started, so they dropped into practice mode and went over some building techniques. Cade was building better than ever, placing floors, ramps, and walls in an easy, systematic rhythm.

"I think today is the day," he said. He seemed to mean it.

"Don't jinx it," Tess warned.

She built up to Cade's structure and shot down one ramp, triggering a chain reaction throughout his entire structure that sent him flying to the ground. She laughed, and on the other end of the voice call, there was only silence. She agreed something felt good about the day. They continued to build and fight each other until it was time to start.

The first two games went similarly to the previous week's competition, and as they waited for the third to begin, they sat in

9th place on the scoreboard. Their combined score was 42. They just had to keep up the momentum for the final game to secure their place in the qualifier.

"What did I say about today?" Cade said. Tess could tell Cade was beaming even though she couldn't see his face.

"We just can't have a repeat of last week," Tess said, though she was to blame for the whole ordeal.

She hadn't been back to therapy, and she hadn't been discussing the manic episode. It was much easier to let it slip to the back of her mind now. Still, for good measure, she had been avoiding the southwest corner of Metropolis where they found the hospital in the first place. She knew those memories were still hiding somewhere, and if she wasn't going to work them out, they wouldn't go away. Still, it was nice to pretend like the whole thing hadn't happened, like perhaps the doctors were wrong about her. As if, maybe, she did not have bipolar disorder after all.

"It's nothing like last week now. I think seeing your friends changed things for you."

Even though that was not the sole reason Tess's mindset had improved, Cade might have had a point. Something in her sparked back to life during that lunch. It had fueled all their games. Cade just didn't know why she'd been in such a bad slump in the first place.

Tess pulled her phone out of her sweatpants pocket, and sure enough, there were messages in the new group chat.

Jordan: Good luck today!
Andrea: You're gonna kill it!
Tara: Maybe become an e-girl just for us, so we can watch.

Tess laughed, but she wasn't going to stream. Having viewers would be an added pressure. She didn't need to worry about that until she was at the Grand Championship—*If* she made it into the Grand Championship—she corrected herself. No need to get cocky yet.

The five-minute timer wound down to zero in the DuskCabins lobby, and Tess prepared for another drop.

"Let's go!" Cade was filled with nothing but excitement and his same endless energy.

Tess huffed with nervousness in return, but she felt, in her heart, that excitement as well. That excitement would be the only emotion left as soon as they jumped off the plane.

Cade followed her out of the plane's cabin, and they dove through the air, plummeting down toward Metropolis. Fueled by a confidence boost from their recent victories, they decided to land directly on the giant tower near the center of town. They waited until the last moment to release their parachutes, ensuring they'd be the first to land on the building. Tess's boots thudded onto the roof first, followed by Cade's, and no one else dared to land with them.

Tess grabbed the uncommon shotgun waiting for her on the sloped surface of the roof, as well as some armor decorating the overlook of the city. Behind her, Cade broke through the stone and dropped to an office below to do his own looting through cubicles.

"I'm going to pick people off in the street. You take anyone else inside," Cade called from below as he walked toward a large window.

Tess was already on her way, dropping down through the hole in the roof and walking toward the staircase. She paused and listened for a moment. Four distinct sets of footsteps were traversing the place. She grinned. This would be a rewarding sweep.

She stalked to the floor below and entered a conference room. Behind two filing cabinets, a zombie-looking man stood with his back turned, reloading a sniper rifle. She took one headshot to knock him to the ground and another to finish him off. Since he had been knocked before disappearing, she knew he had a surviving duo nearby. They were likely on high alert after the loss of their partner.

"Got two!" Cade shouted from above. He was still on the top floor, picking off players on the street.

Tess opened her mouth to call back, only to hear footsteps approaching from the stairs below. It seemed like someone wanted revenge. She closed her mouth and prepared, lining her eyes through her shotgun sight, waiting for his head to rise from the steps onto her level. She took a shot as soon as his head peaked over the staircase, and he was instantly eliminated.

"Got two, too," she called back.

According to her initial analysis, there were at least two more players within the same building, but she couldn't figure out where. She crept to the next floor slowly. A library with a good amount of loot spread out across the shelves.

She carefully maneuvered through every angle of the room, ensuring it was clear, before letting her guard down to take the loot. A standard assault rifle laid flat on the ground and stashed behind some books, a rare rocket launcher.

With closer proximity to the first floor, she could hear the pounding footsteps of the last two players running around the lobby, and from the sound of shots being fired at each other, she inferred they were not on the same team. She needed to swoop in for both kills before their current duel left one dead.

Tess sprinted back to the stairs. As soon as she could see the entrance to the bottom floor, she sent rockets flying into the room. The explosion blasted red and orange fire in every direction, sending furniture scraps flying through the room. Both players were eliminated instantly.

"Building's cleared," she called as she gathered some armor the opponents had left behind. It still gleamed in perfect condition atop the rubble.

"I've got another on the north street...one more shot, and he is dead."

Tess scanned the street outside a shattered window on the north side of the room and spotted the player Cade was talking about. He cowered behind some trash cans, barely clinging to life. She took out her own assault rifle and aimed. One shot took him down.

"Good shit," Cade said, and she felt a surge of adrenaline at the praise. "I saw more people in the northwest side of town. I'm going to make my way over on the roofs, you stay down low. We can close in on their building from both sides."

They worked their way through Metropolis, closing in on the other duos until the entire town was cleared. By the time they were finished, their kill count had risen to thirteen, and the zone was pushing in.

Tess unfolded a map from her pack on a diner table. It showed that the final circle would surround the farmland, which would mean a lot of building fights. Tess was delighted but apprehensive for Cade. Even with his improvements, he got overconfident at times.

They encountered three more duos as they made their way across hilly terrain. They took down each team with ease and brought their score up to nineteen.

"I'd say a win will guarantee our placement," Cade said. He weaved through thick rose bushes just ahead of Tess. The words didn't seem to hold real weight yet, as she was still lost from the outside world, so engrossed in the match.

"There are two duos left. I say don't count your chickens 'til they're cooked."

"What?"

"I think I said it wrong."

They both started laughing, but the chuckles faded as they neared the farmland. An enormous building fight towered above Cade and Tess. Wood was meshed into metal and twisted into cobblestone. It was a nonsensical structure, larger than Tess had ever seen.

"Tess, I have an idea."

"Oh no." She smirked.

They crouched behind a fallen tree, staring up at the building, which looked like something from a Dr. Seuss book.

"You remember earlier in practice how you knocked down my structure by shooting just one ramp?" Cade asked.

Tess glanced back at Cade, an eyebrow raised. "Yes."

"And you've still got the rockets, right?"

"Yes." A grin formed on her face as she realized what he was thinking.

"Let's light up the bottom of their structures, and they'll all come tumbling down."

He ran ahead with his assault rifle, spraying at the ramps that served as the base for the massive build fight. Tess snapped into action shortly after, following up with her rockets.

"ALL OF THEM!" Cade shouted.

"I'm trying!" She laughed again.

Wood fragments flew through the sky as each shot collided with the structure's base holding the four remaining players. The other duos were so engrossed in their own battle that they didn't even try to contest Cade or Tess as they tore through the base.

Tess's gaze lurched toward the sky after the last piece of the foundation was destroyed. Like falling dominos, the rest of the pieces began to automatically shatter, and the four remaining players plummeted to the ground, accompanied by satisfying thuds. They died instantly, and the screen changed.

VICTORY: BLACKLANTERN AND JUSTATESST

There was a stunned silence on both ends of the voice call. Tess quickly backed out to the lobby to check where their final game had placed them on the scoreboard. All Tess could see on her screen was the refresh symbol.

"Come on," she breathed.

"THIRD PLACE TESS!" Cade hollered from his end of the call.

Tess placed a hand on her desk as she tried to steady her body. "No way," she whispered. It was hard to speak. Hard to breathe.

Finally, the refresh symbol disappeared, and she could see the scoreboard. There they were: BlackLantern and JustATesss, ranked third out of 52,400 duos.

"Cade, we are going!"

She placed her other hand over her mouth. Perhaps she was entering shock, but she had believed this would happen all along, hadn't she? It turned out that believing something would happen and actually watching it unfold were entirely different sensations.

"HELL YEAH, WE ARE GOING! Tess, you're a god! I'm a god! We deserve this. We put in the hours. Now, we get to compete side by side!"

If the victory hadn't already sent her into shock, she was certain that statement had. Tess didn't know if she felt ready to meet Cade face to face. Suddenly, the problems she had with her complexion and body felt very loud.

Would their duo still be as foolproof once she met Cade in person? Would it complicate things?

Cade rambled on without a worry in the world, "I'm going to buy us a nice dinner to celebrate this game! Just two weeks from now, when we are really there."

Tess wondered what it felt like to be inside Cade's head. She was aware she was overthinking again, but that didn't mean she could just turn it off. What did it feel like to not constantly drown in your own worry?

"I'm holding you to that," she attempted to sound nonchalant.

"Tess, you're supposed to be screaming with me! Say 'WOOH!'"

She laughed, "I am not saying that."

"Damnit, Tess, we just won in the sickest way possible. You owe it to me."

She glanced around the room nervously. "Alright...wooh."

"More passion!" he demanded.

"WOoh!" she yelled.

"There we go! That's my duo!" They both laughed. "I could kiss you," Cade added. Tess froze. He'd never flirted with her in such a direct way.

"You could in two weeks," she spoke before considering the words leaving her mouth.

"Could I?" he mused, his voice so frustratingly calm.

Before she could respond, a notification popped on her screen, stealing her attention.

Congratulations JustaTesst! SpersaGames will contact you shortly regarding your qualification for the Grand Championship!

"Better be ready for that phone call," Cade said. "Let's give ourselves a break for the rest of the day to celebrate."

Tess quickly agreed and closed the game. She had to tell her family and friends. They were going to freak out. She began to walk out of the room, but her cell phone started ringing. It was an unknown number—she was sure it belonged to the group hosting the Grand Championship, SpersaGames.

Chapter Thirteen
Headshots

"Three games and fifteen dollars. That's my final offer."

Tess stood with her arms crossed outside of her thirteen-year-old brother's room. Inside, Daniel sat slumped on top of a blue bean bag chair, surrounded by what looked like the aftermath of a clothing tornado. Tess didn't dare cross into the disaster zone, lest the smell of dirty socks get any worse.

"Three games and twenty dollars," Daniel bargained without looking up, fingers flicking across an Xbox controller, his tongue sticking out as he finished a game of DuskCabins.

Tess let out an exasperated sigh. "Fine."

A wide grin spread across Daniel's face. "I would have done it for ten."

Tess rolled her eyes. "Come over to my room when you're done with your game."

"Okay," Daniel called back.

Tess made her way across the hall. Damned headshots. She didn't have any recent pictures of herself, and the ones she did have included other people. Always laying across the couch between Tara and Jordan. Andrea was usually the one behind the camera insisting they "memorialize the moment". Well, if only they had memorialized the moment in high quality close up to Tess's face one of those times. Then she wouldn't be out twenty bucks.

Inside her room, her computer was open to DuskCabins. She left it running most of the time in case Cade randomly logged on for some games. Plus, the music and graphics were comforting in a way she didn't like to admit. She closed her eyes and listened to the lobby music. It was interrupted about three times with notifications. Three more friend requests.

"Why can't you just automatically decline those?" she muttered to the nonexistent DuskCabins secretary.

Her friend list had exploded since they qualified for the tournament. They started playing anonymously to avoid further recognition.

The exposure went far beyond video games. Tess had to make all her social media private. Her direct message requests were full, ranging from supportive gamers to desperate men and the occasional trolls. She tried to avoid the online feedback as much as possible. Most of it wasn't negative, but it was too overwhelming.

"I'm ready," Daniel said. He stood at the entrance to Tess's room with his iPhone in hand.

"Let's make it quick," Tess replied, rising from the bed with a sigh.

She glanced at herself in the mirror. She had done simple makeup and was wearing a plain black t-shirt. Nothing too distracting or over the top. Crossing the room, she leaned against her white door.

"Will this work?" she asked.

"How am I supposed to know?" Daniel replied, glancing back into the hall as if during the time she was deciding on a backdrop he could be curing rare diseases back in his room.

"Well, does it look distracting?" Tess asked.

"It looks plain," he shrugged and swiped on his phone to bring up the camera. He stepped back a few feet and then looked through the screen. "You said it had to be from your shoulders up?"

"Yep, that should be good." Tess glanced down and smoothed the bottom of her shirt, even though it likely wouldn't make the photo.

"Alright, done." Daniel said.

Tess's head snapped back up. "What?"

"I'm done with the picture," he answered.

Tess crossed her arms. "I didn't even smile."

Daniel groaned. "Okay, fine. I'll take it again."

Tess didn't waste any time before forcing a magazine ready smile onto her face. Her smile faltered as she thought maybe she should have gone professional for this. Still, she didn't want to waste money right now, not with no guarantee of placing at the Grand Championship. Besides, what else were siblings for? She perked the smile back up.

"Okay, now I'm done," Daniel said

Tess walked over as her brother brought up the photo gallery. "Show me."

He swiped through a few shots. She nearly grabbed the phone out of his hands just to delete a couple where she was glaring at him. He swiped to the end and then back to the beginning. Tess weighed the torment of taking more and settled for one of the last few where she was actually smiling. Close enough. Her brother sent them over to her phone.

"The qualifier is at two, so let's do our three games now," Daniel said.

"Alright," Tess agreed, and she walked back into her room, sitting down in front of the PC.

Daniel had it in his head that if Tess could make it into the Grand Championship, so could he and his best friend Eric. Who was she to disagree? Throughout the week he begged Tess to give him lessons and insight. At first it was sort of fun. Her little brother had never wanted to play with her so much before. But at this point, she kind of missed it being that way.

Cade appeared inside the party and Tess inhaled sharply. "I didn't think you were getting on for another hour," she said.

"It's nice to see you too," Cade replied.

Tess shook her head, realizing how that must have sounded. "No, it's just—"

"I'm ready!" Daniel called excitedly as he joined the party.

Tess sighed. She was not planning on doing introductions along with the lessons. She closed her eyes as if she could will her brother not to embarrass her with telepathy.

"No way! You're that guy my sister's obsessed with."
Telepathy failed.

Tess swooped in before he could do any further damage.
"Yes, Daniel. Cade is the guy that I duo with."

Cade burst out laughing on his end. Tess winced; he was
laughing a little too hard.

"I think your brother had it right the first time," he said
eventually.

"Regardless," Tess said, attempting to regain her composure,
"I promised Daniel I would coach him for three games. He's
hoping to qualify for the tournament with his friend Eric today.
So, if you don't mind, Cade, I can text you when we're done
and—"

"I want BlackLantern to help with the coaching," Daniel
said.

Tess lightly slapped her palm on her face. As if being on the
call with both her brother and Cade had not buried her enough
into a deep hole of shame within a singular minute, now he
wanted Cade to stick around longer.

"I'd love to show you a few things," Cade said. Tess could
hear pride bleeding through Cade's voice. Her brother not only
managed to throw her under the bus, but also to boost Cade's ego
right before their practice. Something she would have to deal with
for the rest of the day.

Still, it seemed like she was not left with much of a choice.
"Looks like we are playing some trio games," Tess said, caving in.

Two games later, Tess trailed behind Cade and her brother—
who was literally skipping—through a dense jungle. The two had
become a little too buddy-buddy, teaming up to veto Tess's target
destinations for the most ludicrous drops. Tess glanced behind
her shoulder as the zone closed in behind them, hissing. A deep
red storm swallowing up any stragglers in its path.

"I told you to take the SMG over the rifle back there," Cade said, pushing aside a vine for Daniel "because we're going to end up in close combat at the hedge maze."

Tess caught the vine as it swung back towards her and tailed them quietly. Overhead, a few monkeys crawled through the trees, dropping bananas in their path. The bananas bounced down onto seafoam mushrooms clinging to the side of thick rainforest trees and then onto the ground.

"Eat one of those," Tess called ahead to Daniel. "They'll heal you for a tiny bit."

Daniel paused, picked up a banana, and munched on it slowly as Cade parted the foliage up ahead. Light spilled into the dark jungle. He squinted toward the mansion, where the final zone was closing. The backyard was a swarm of hedged bushes creating a massive, intricate maze.

"The final duo is camped on either end of the maze," Cade said, letting the foliage fall back in place. He turned back to Tess and Daniel. "Tess and I will keep pressure from a distance, and you can go in for the kills."

Daniel stared at Cade in awe. "Wait, I will fight both of them?"

"That's what it takes to make it pro," Cade said, like he'd already been signed to a major Esports team. Tess rolled her eyes, but she knew with the pressure they could keep, it would be a breeze for Daniel.

"I can do it," Daniel said firmly. He tossed his banana peel aside.

Cade nodded with a small grin and opened the foliage again. "Go for it."

Daniel sprinted out of the jungle toward the hedge maze like a mad man, while Tess and Cade built themselves a sniper tower on the edge of the zone. They peered into the maze from above and watched with a clear view of Daniel's path from their vantage point. He was approaching the first player. Cade exchanged a glance with Tess, and then they both peppered the enemy a couple of times with their assault rifles.

"Turn left with your SMG ready," Cade instructed Daniel.

Daniel raised the gun into the air and turned the corner slowly, finishing the player with a few easy sprays. Tess spotted his duo on the other side of the maze. He began to build up above the hedge, responding to his downed partner. Tess had to fight her instinct to take out her sniper rifle and finish him off with just one shot.

"Build up," she said to Daniel.

He started stacking a few awkward ramps into the sky. Tess narrowed her eyes. The opponent lined up a shot, preparing to take Dainel's structure down. Before she could pull her own trigger, Cade shot the opponent in the shoulder, knocking him off balance.

"One more shot," Cade called.

Daniel sprayed his gun but was not connecting a single shot. It was too hard for him to land them at this distance.

"New Plan," Tess muttered. She sprayed down the opponent's ramps, forcing him to drop back into the maze. She hesitated again, fighting the urge to finish the player off completely. "Jump over the hedge and turn right," she told Daniel. Then she started shooting behind the player, forcing their path toward where she had told Daniel to go.

He turned the corner to face Daniel, who stood at the ready with his SMG. After Daniel sprayed him once in the head, he faded into the void and the victory message displayed on the screen.

VICTORY: LEGENDWOLF, BLACKLANTERN, AND JUSTATESST

Her brother was shrieking with joy on his end of the call, completely enthused to have clutched the game. Tess winced at the high pitch. She knew where the nickname 'squeakers' came from all too well—it was a nickname for prepubescent gamers.

"Let's go brother!" Cade shouted.

"And that's three," Tess said, a little too excited to have her liability out of the party. To be fair Daniel hadn't said anything too damaging since his first comment, but who knew what else would come out with time.

"Good luck with the tournament," Cade said.

"Thanks. Cool to meet you!" Daniel said, and with that he left the party.

Tess exhaled and slumped back in her chair. With her brother gone, they could finally focus on preparing for the Grand Championship.

"I've got to admit, I've been a little nervous for New York," Cade said after a moment.

Tess blinked. "You have?"

Maybe she wasn't the only one unsure of how things would play out in person. She wondered if something about playing with her brother had triggered the vulnerability from Cade's end.

"Still," Cade continued, "I'm going to power through for my biggest fans. I heard some of them are obsessed with me."

Of course, Cade being vulnerable for possibly the first time ever was just an elaborate set up to a joke.

"Let's get to the wagers," Tess said flatly, refusing to indulge him.

Still, she wondered if there was any truth to Cade's initial comment, or if she was the only one with nerves as the Grand Championship approached—unsure what complications meeting offline would bring.

Chapter Fourteen
Pre-Departure

"You should pack this shirt for New York, you'll fit right in," Tara said, standing in front of Tess's closet two weeks after her qualification. She had insisted on advising her wardrobe after seeing the mass amount of media attention Tess was receiving.

"It's cute," Tess agreed. She stuck out her arms, and Tara threw it over to her.

Tess sat cross-legged on her bedroom floor, her carry-on suitcase open wide next to her. She rolled the shirt and placed it inside. At the bottom of her suitcase, her lithium was packed in a bright orange container, along with other medications.

She frowned as she covered the pill bottles with the shirt. Lately, Tess had been feeling so good that she started to doubt that she would need the medication for the rest of her life, despite what the doctors had told her. Relying on something like that when everything felt fine was a strange, uncomfortable contradiction.

"And this skirt to match! I can see you in the interviews now—Oh my god!" Without waiting for a response, Tara flung the plaid miniskirt at Tess's face, momentarily blocking her view of the room.

Tess laughed and tugged it off her face. "Good thing my reflexes are better inside the game."

She and Cade continued to practice every night, pushing for higher scores. Sometimes, it went better, sometimes worse. Their communication was solid, but the aggressive playstyle always came with a risk.

"Why'd you turn down the local interviews?" Tara asked. She spoke carefully, but an edge in her tone made it seem like she'd been building up to this question all along.

Tess's hands paused, and she dropped the skirt in her lap, it unrolled instantly. She glanced in her bag, where she had covered the medication. "I'm afraid of what might come out."

"What do you mean by that?" Tara moved to the edge of the bed and sat down. "Sorry to break it to you, but the headlines already talk about how you are a girl. The cat's out of the bag."

Tess and Cade were the highlights of every gaming news channel covering the DuskCabins Grand Championship. She was the only girl to qualify for the tournament, and the media was eating up the story of her friendship with Cade—how they had yet to meet. Besides that, they stood out as the underdogs because they weren't sponsored by a professional team. They were independents that made it into the Grand Championship, which was rare.

"I like how people see me right now," Tess said. "I stand out as the only girl in the tournament. That's what makes me different. What I'm scared of is for my recent life to get out and then stand out as the mentally ill player in the tournament. I don't want to be known for doing all this despite the bipolar stuff. I just want to be known for doing it."

"You don't have to share anything about your health that you don't want to. That's your business," Tara said firmly.

"I know. It's just... I worry it'll slip out somehow if I do interviews. Or maybe someone who knows about it will sell them the story, and I will be cornered with questions I'm not ready to answer." Tess frowned and looked at her lap. "I want to control my own narrative, but I also don't want to tell that story yet. I'm not ready myself, and without the therapy..." her voice trailed off.

Tess felt guilty for stopping the sessions so suddenly. It was the only place she had been able to open up, but returning didn't seem like an option. The video game competition was the most fun she'd had her entire life, and she didn't want to sabotage it.

Was therapy really progress anyway if it just made her feel worse? Bringing all those memories to the surface, reliving the mania inside her head she longed to forget. It didn't seem healthy to keep returning to that episode.

"Have you told Cade about it?" Tara tilted her head. Her tone was innocent, but Tess felt her head begin to pound.

"I thought you said I don't have to share if I don't want to," Tess replied sharply.

Tara flinched. "You don't. I was just wondering. I'm sorry...it's none of my business."

Tess exhaled and relaxed her body. She picked the skirt back off her lap and rolled it again. "No, I'm sorry. I just feel defensive about that. Cade and I have a good rhythm right now and I don't want that to complicate it."

That being the details they seemed to want to keep to themselves. If things were to get complicated another way, she wouldn't mind as much.

"You guys definitely have a rhythm," Tara smirked, her mind seemed to be in the same place. She walked back to the closet and resumed rummaging through the options.

Tess opened her mouth to argue, but the words still rang in the back of her mind. *I could kiss you.*

"I haven't been with anyone...like romantically...since everything happened," Tess said suddenly.

Tara held up a baby blue maxi dress. "This dress is super cute, too." She didn't seem too surprised by Tess's statement, which only furthered Tess's anxiety.

"Tara, I mean it! It's been months."

"Tess, it's natural. It'll come back to you if it's meant to be." Tara folded the dress carefully as if it was made of glass. It was gorgeous silk, purchased on a trip to Florida with Andrea right after high school. Tess had never had the right occasion to wear it.

Tara walked over to Tess and sat across from her on the floor, placing the folded dress inside the suitcase. It stood out, contrasting the simple rolled clothes Tess had added like its beauty didn't belong there.

"Tess," she said quietly, "you know you're beautiful, right?"

Tess blinked, caught off guard, and then laughed.

But Tara didn't laugh. Her expression remained serious. "I mean it, Tess. I can tell that what happened with your manic episode shook you, but you're still the most gorgeous, confident, enemy-slaying gamer girl, who still won't stream for me, that I know."

"That was far too many adjectives," Tess replied flatly.

Tara stuck out her tongue in response. Then she narrowed her eyebrows, eyes typically as welcoming as a puppy, turned fierce like a panther. "I'm just saying, if Cade doesn't respect you or know your worth, I swear I'll—"

Tess waved her hand, flagging Tara to stop. "Alright, calm down over there. He does respect me, and I think he knows my worth. It's at least fifty thousand dollars for simply competing."

Her expression didn't let up. "I mean beyond that…"

"He sees it beyond that too, Tara. I can tell."

Her playful grin returned, and she shifted back. "Well then, what are you so worried about? You're beautiful. He treats you well. And you're going to slay the competition! Most importantly, your health is your business, and you're allowed to keep it that way."

Tess felt so much comfort in the way Tara described her. She wished her friend could come along to New York with her. But no one could get off work, so Tess was making the journey solo. At least everyone would still be able to watch as the tournament was streamed.

Tara's mouth gaped open, and Tess tensed in alarm, trying to figure out what could possibly be wrong.

"Dear god…we haven't packed any jewelry."

Before Tess could blink, Tara was back on her feet en route to the dresser, where Tess stored her limited jewelry collection. Tess rolled her eyes but followed her friend over.

It was hard to believe that by this time tomorrow, she would be at the hotel in New York, and it was even harder to believe that by this time tomorrow she'd be hearing Cade's voice outside of a headset.

Chapter Fifteen
Room Service, Anyone?

When Tess landed in New York, a kind middle-aged man who she had sat next to on the plane helped her pull her bag down from the overhead compartment. She thanked him and then quickly turned her phone off airplane mode. She opened the email with instructions that she'd already read through six times.

A SpersaGames representative was supposed to wait for her outside the landing area. They would have a sign with her name on it. Weirdly, the directions hadn't magically changed the sixth time she read it, but you could never be too careful.

A text loaded in. It would have came in an hour ago if Tess had not had her data turned off.

Cade: I just landed. Let me know what room you're in when you get here.

Tess felt her heart begin to pound. For a while this trip didn't feel like something that was actually going to happen. Now she had to face the reality that she was about to meet Cade. She closed the message, unready to respond and tugged at her DuskCabins t-shirt nervously—her grandmother had bought it for her despite not truly understanding what she was doing.

As she stepped off the plane, she tried to savor the last slow moments she would have before she was swallowed up in the competitive gaming world. She felt a sense of calm in being a part of a crowd of people, all hurried to their own different destinations. Advertisements for the Grand Championship were on pillars throughout the airport, and she found it surreal that she and Cade were competing in such a massive event.

After exiting the restricted airport area, she immediately identified the SpersaGames staff member waiting for her. A woman stood across the room, her uniform matching the logo, and she held a sign reading 'Tess'. Standing beside her, a group of children excitedly scanned the room. They were accompanied by a few tired-looking adults who stood behind them.

One of the younger girls with yellow bobbing pigtails caught her eye, glanced at her shirt, and squealed, "Tess!"

The group erupted into cheers, and Tess didn't have to force the grin as she approached.

"Hi, Tess!" the staff member greeted her warmly, "I'm Adrian, and I'll be working with you throughout the tournament. I'm sure you are tired from traveling, as I told this group."

"Hi," Tess replied. She didn't know where to look; there were so many different eyes on her. The children were peering up in excitement, Adrian in sympathy, and the parents were taking her in skeptically.

A young boy stepped forward, holding out his phone. "Can we take a photo together?"

Tess glanced back at Adrian, who simply shrugged. It seemed it was up to her. She looked back at the parents, and one of the adults smiled at her sympathetically.

"They've been waiting for you for an hour," she explained.

"Well, of course we can!" Tess said.

She abandoned her luggage on the ground and, one by one, took a photo with each of the children. It felt funny that anyone would have waited for her, especially since she had avoided interviews up to this point. But at the same time, she sheepishly remembered herself waiting outside a Paramore concert, praying that Hayley Williams would walk by afterward. It was hard to believe that the kids possibly admired her similarly.

After the group was satisfied, Tess followed Adrian out of the airport and into a taxi.

"There's going to be a lot of kids like that around the stadium," Adrian warned as she took the taxi's front seat.

"I don't know if I have the energy for all that," Tess admitted, resting her head against the cool window.

Adrian laughed. She turned her body to face Tess in the backseat. "I think you'll find the energy, just like you do for those matches. I saw the playthrough of your last qualifier with Cade. The way you ended that match was great!"

"Thanks," Tess replied, flustered. She hadn't expected someone from SpersaGames to have actually watched her gameplay. The compliment felt different coming from someone who knew the game as well as she did.

"We have you staying at the Hills Inn. It's a five-minute taxi ride from the stadium." Adrian lurched forward as the cab honked and swerved around traffic. She turned back around as if nothing happened a moment later. "Cade's already checked in. He flew in this morning."

Tess's stomach did a somersault. She was not ready to think about seeing him yet. She tried to focus on the skyscrapers they whirred by in the taxi.

"Tonight, you can get settled in. The events won't start until tomorrow," Adrian continued. "I'll meet you at the stadium to show you our practice facilities. We'll provide lunch for all the duos, and in the afternoon, we have a meet-and-greet with VIP guests.

"Sunday, of course, is the competition, starting in the early afternoon, with time to warm up all morning."

As Adrian spoke, Tess was trying to commit the whole schedule to memory. It sounded like it was going to be a lot.

Adrian must have picked up on her panicked expression. "Don't worry. I have a schedule for you in your room and a little care package. I'll also give you my business card, you can contact me if you need anything."

The taxi slowed and pulled next to the curb in front of a luxurious hotel. Tess stepped out onto the sidewalk. She did a slow turn to take in the atmosphere of New York. The hotel sat on the edge of Central Park, where people dressed for all sorts of occasions were milling about. The smell…wasn't great. Something like sewage water mixed with pizza. Still, there was no denying the city hummed with energy.

"It's amazing," she murmured.

The taxi driver dropped Tess's luggage by her side, and Adrian gestured toward the hotel's entrance. Inside, the lobby was covered with dark green ivy and plush purple furniture. To the right, there was a small bar where a few guests sat and chatted on the velvet barstools over cocktails. Tess scanned the stools for Cade but didn't catch a match for the Venmo photo she'd practically memorized.

A man approached from the front desk; his white suit sleeve pulled back as he held out a small envelope. "Hello, you must be Tess. You will be in room 301. Please let us know if there's anything else we can assist with." He turned to nod at Adrian, who returned the gesture with a smile.

"Thanks," Tess mustered, still in awe of the hotel's architecture and interior decoration. A small waterfall protruded from the left wall into a stone basin. She had never stayed somewhere so elegant in her life.

"The elevators are back there." Adrian, who didn't seem quite as fazed, nodded toward a smaller hallway with decorative artwork. She retrieved a black business card from her pocket. "Here is my card. I'll see you tomorrow!"

Tess grinned as she took the card and went down the hallway. She stepped into a golden metal elevator, and a couple followed her inside. She studied the golden bracelets dangling from the wrist of a pretty young woman. The way she decorated her wrist appeared to be worth more than Tess had made in her entire life. Tess pulled out her phone and replied to Cade's earlier message.

Tess: I landed, and I'm headed to room 301 to unpack. See you soon.

The elevator dinged open on the third floor, and Tess stepped into the hallway. Her room was the first to the left of the hall. She swiped her card and pushed open the door. The interior was beautiful, the bed covered in a purple satin comforter and the same ivy lining the walls. Yet the room was petite; this was certainly New York. On top of the bed was a welcome basket stuffed with snacks, a folder, and a golden plush DuskCabins shotgun. She picked it up and squeezed the trigger.

"Cute."

She laughed at the absurdity of a plush gun and then opened the folder. Inside were more details about her stay and copies of the paperwork she'd filled out for SpersaGames. At the bottom, folded neatly in plastic, was her very own jersey. It was accompanied by a note instructing her to wear it on Sunday.

She pressed the plastic to her chest and squeezed, unable to believe this was her reality. Her eyes drifted to the window, a portal to a collection of skyscrapers and pedestrians. She smiled when she noticed a coffee shop to the far right of the block.

A knock at the door startled Tess from her personal bedroom tour. She nervously patted down her hair and tugged at her t-shirt. She wasn't ready to meet Cade yet. The knock sounded again, firmer this time. And yet, she was going to have to answer that door.

She made her way across the room, sucking in the butterflies that tumbled around her stomach. She slowly opened the door, attempting to keep her face neutral.

"Hello ma'am. I've got your gourmet pizza."

Tess's face dropped. It was room service. "Uh—no…sorry, I don't think it's for me."

Surprised, the man blinked and pulled a small booklet from his pocket. "My mistake, ma'am. It's for 501."

"It's alright!" she replied, beaming with relief. The man looked confused; he had probably never seen someone so happy about a disturbance.

"I'll be on my way then." He pushed his cart back down the hall. Tess nervously glanced to the left and right to make sure no one else was approaching before closing the door.

She turned to unpack her carry-on, stripping off her sweatpants and t-shirt in exchange for jeans and the cute top that

Tara had insisted upon. She fixed her eyeliner in the mirror and sank into the desk chair to review all the materials SpersaGames had left.

There was another knock.

"I didn't order anything," Tess called. She flipped a page in the packet and began skimming the bios of other competitors.

"Does that mean you're not hungry?"

Her heart stopped. She would recognize that voice anywhere, headset or not.

She dropped the papers and took a steadying breath before stepping across the room to open the door. Cade was standing nonchalantly outside. His broad figure filled out a blue flannel shirt with thin white stripes. He was wearing khakis and spotless plain white sneakers. His warm brown eyes stared right down at Tess into her own.

"Well, that's not fair," Tess said, looking up at him. "You didn't tell me you were tall."

His whole face lit up as he laughed, and Tess had to look away as she started to grin herself. His smile was like a magnetic force filling the atmosphere, begging you to join it. The dimples formed just like in his photograph.

He wasn't that tall, hovering only a few inches above her. She just couldn't think of anything else to say. When she looked back, he was still staring at her and ran a hand through his scruffy brown hair. It was weird to see him here as a three-dimensional, moving person. She had only imagined him in 2D by his picture on Venmo.

He moved toward her, and she instinctively stepped back, but he didn't react. He just continued to walk past her into the room. He picked up the plush toy from her basket. "They got you a plush shotgun? Mine was a sniper rifle." He glanced at the open paperwork spread across the table of her small room. "And you're already in business mode, I see."

She hadn't moved from the entrance, startled by how calm and confident he was, just like in the games. He acted like this wasn't the first time they met face to face. How was he not facing the same shock as her?

Suddenly, she remembered the pill bottles in her open carry-on laid out and open on the ground. He hadn't noticed them yet. She moved carefully to close the bag while he scanned her paperwork. He didn't seem to notice exactly what she was doing, but he did become self-conscious at her careful body language.

"I'm sorry," Cade said, turning back with a slight frown. "I just came barging right in."

"It's fine," Tess reassured him quickly. "That's the exact aggression I want to see from you in the tournament on Sunday." She glanced from him to her bed, still perfectly made. "You wanted to get food, right?"

As he followed her gaze, Cade seemed lost in thought but snapped out of it at the word 'food'. "Yes, I want to treat you to a nice place, like I promised."

"You said a lot of things..." Tess began, her voice quieter now. Were they going to have that conversation right now?

"One thing at a time, Tess." He smirked at her forwardness, and she felt the heat rise in her face as she took in his maddeningly smug expression.

"I knew you were blushy."

"Shut up! You couldn't have known that."

"Sometimes a guy can tell." Cade grinned. "The place is nice, and I have a reservation for seven. It's a few blocks away."

She glanced at her phone. It was six. "Well, I'm going to need to change. And I was thinking we can research the competition a bit more—try to learn their playstyles."

They had started looking into their competitors when the final list was revealed a few days prior.

"Good idea. I've got a list of the players in my room, too."

"Come back a little before seven, then?"

"What, no handshake or anything first?" Cade asked. He was closing the distance between them, but Tess stood her ground nervously. He stopped just an inch away from her. He smelled like sea salt and cologne. He extended his hand, and she raised hers to meet his rough, warm grip.

"It's great doing business with you." She attempted to sound corporate.

Cade laughed and tugged his arm back, pulling her body forward with it until it collided with his own. He wrapped both of his arms around her. Her body leaned into him before she even realized what she was doing.

"A pleasure," he murmured so casually that she almost would not believe that her body was pressed against his if she couldn't feel his heartbeat racing. Maybe there were some nerves under that exterior, after all.

His touch was light, like soft rain, the kind she'd sat and watched so carefully from the windows as a child, but also charged like the vibrant lightning that lit up the sky. As a child, she hated the thunder that would shortly follow. Yet, somehow miraculously, there was only the soft rain and lightning in this simple hug. No sign of thunder.

It was over in a moment, and Cade stepped back, gave her one last smile, and slipped out the door. Tess returned to getting ready, wondering what would be their thunder? For even if she dreaded it, she knew with rain and lighting, it was never too far behind.

Chapter Sixteen
A Night in NYC

An hour later, Tess had learned there was a lot to be nervous about.

For one, the competition was going to be fierce. As expected, every duo dropped high-kill games like Tess and Cade. The majority were represented by professional leagues, but a few others were independent. There were fifty duos total, so a hundred players would be dropped into the same match three times.

Another focus of Tess's worry was that she'd decided to wear the blue silk dress Tara had added to her suitcase. Tess wondered how strongly she'd stand out as they walked through Manhattan.

The shadow cast by the former issue of the tournament was large enough to calm Tess's nerves regarding the dress, for now at least.

Cade knocked.

She gathered her nerves then walked out the door and didn't pause to watch his reaction. She wasn't sure she could handle it. "Where are we headed?"

"Two blocks south. It's an Italian place." Cade brushed past her to take the lead, his phone open to the Maps application. He touched her dress as he walked by. "This is lovely."

With a reddened face, she followed him down to the lobby, where the staff greeted them once again. Cade struck up a brief conversation about the restaurant. Tess admired the way that he held himself in conversation. He still seemed as cocky as ever, but somehow approachable and charming. He listened intently while the other person spoke—it seemed like he had the ability to make others feel heard.

She glanced around the lobby. If it weren't for the dressy clothes, she and Cade might have looked out of place here. He wore a solid blue collared shirt with formal black pants and the same white shoes from earlier. The light blue color contrasted beautifully against his sun-tanned skin. There wasn't a wrinkle in sight—he seemed to have ironed it—which caught Tess by surprise.

Her thoughts were interrupted as Cade's fingers interlaced with her own. "This way, JustATesst."

She rolled her eyes but didn't pull away from the grip. She thought she could handle following directions without getting lost, but as they made their way out onto a New York street that had become much busier with the night, she felt comfort in his grasp. Midtown Manhattan was exactly as she'd heard it described. Chaotic and magical all at once.

"What were you talking about?" she asked Cade as they walked side by side along the city sidewalk. She hadn't really paid attention to the conversation; she just stood awkwardly to the side, taking in the surroundings.

"The restaurant. He recommended the seafood alfredo," he replied.

She dropped his hand as they shuffled into a single-file line to get past a group of teenagers, taking up most of the sidewalk. She missed his touch already.

"I love seafood!" Tess called ahead over the noisy atmosphere.

"I remember you mentioned it before," Cade replied, glancing back.

She studied him for a moment. She hadn't expected him to remember such a minuscule thing unrelated to the gameplay. He took in the surrounding buildings and looked at his phone to compare the directions. The streetlights casted a soft light across his face, and she noticed faint freckles scattered across his focused expression.

"Then how is it you can never remember," she said, returning to his side, "I prefer stun grenades over damage grenades every time?"

She looked at him expectantly but had to glance away when he met her gaze. She knew her anxiety was obvious, but he didn't point it out or let it affect their conversation.

"I remember, instead, which of us knows how to use the stun grenades effectively."

Tess looked back to his face and opened her mouth in a fake offended expression. Cade started laughing, his face lit up again. She supposed most people did, but she had never imagined it quite right for him over the mic. She playfully shoved him, and his right shoulder hit a street sign. He shot her a look, and she struggled to suppress her grin.

"That's been a long time coming," she teased. "How much further?"

Cade rolled his eyes with a playful grin. "It's just around this corner."

They turned the corner and stopped before a small Italian restaurant nestled between looming steel buildings. The peach walls stood out strongly against the gray of New York's skyscrapers. Green ivy grew down the sides of the walls, much like that of their hotel. Tess glanced down at herself; she had forgotten she was dressed well enough to be at a place like this.

"Well, this is definitely different from hot dogs," Tess said simply.

Cade laughed. "We can have hot dogs tomorrow. Come on."

He grabbed her hand again and pulled her inside.

"I guess I'm going to have to get used to that," she said playfully.

"Can't be too careful; it's easy to get lost in a place like this." He shrugged, with a charming smile. Her heart only melted in the slightest.

The entrance was small and warmly lit, decorated in golden tones. Cade stepped ahead and confirmed their reservation with the host. They were guided to a table in the back corner, next to a window with a street view: a picturesque scene—construction and angry pedestrians.

"So," Cade said as they sat, "tell me about yourself."

Tess laughed. "You act like we've never met."

There was something so easy about talking to him. It contradicted the weird feeling that Cade, as a person, was a stranger to her.

"We haven't. Technically."

He took a sip of water and Tess felt a chill run up her spine as his eyes lingered on her appearance. It was like he was truly seeing her for the first time. "Is this what you wear every time we play together?" he asked.

"More like sweats and a T-shirt," Tess replied. "But I figured I'd grace you with something more put together if we were going all out on dinner." She flashed a customer service smile to hide the way her heart pounded, but she could never control the blush that would spread to her face.

"Same here." Cade raised his water cup like he was toasting before taking another sip.

The waiter came by, and Tess ordered the seafood alfredo, following the staff's recommendation. Cade ordered a chicken pasta dish instead.

"What was the first shooter game you ever played?" Cade asked after the waiter left.

"Now that's an interesting question."

Tess thought about it. She had grown up on cheap games that her family rented from Blockbuster—they weren't exactly shooters. That was until her uncle introduced her to—

"I played Call of Duty first," Tess said. Cade nodded, seeming to agree this was a good shooter game. "But I played it on the Wii."

He choked on his water as he started laughing, and Tess chuckled back at him, magnetized by his own laughter. "Thank God you switched to PC," he said between laughs. "Imagine playing in the tournament tomorrow on a Wii controller."

"I think I could still out-build you," Tess insisted with a smirk.

"Oh, there she goes. You've always gotta be mean." He gave her a fake pout, and Tess laughed, but he had a point.

She looked down at her plate for a moment. "I'm sorry. I just can't help it sometimes."

Cade smiled softly and then looked thoughtful for a moment. His expression turned devious. "Let's try a fun game."

"What kind of game?" Tess leaned in curiously. She loved games if there was a way to win.

"Let's say one nice thing about each other."

Her body deflated. So, this wasn't a game she could win.

"Oh, come on. Get that look off your face," Cade said, rolling his eyes.

She put her hands over her face momentarily. She hadn't even been aware she was giving him a look.

"I preferred conversing with the headset—when we couldn't see each other's facial expression," she joked, peeking through her hands before she lowered them back to her side.

"Don't lie." His lips quirked up.

"You have very good strategic thinking," she muttered, eyes drifting toward the window.

"Sorry? Louder, please." He leaned back in his chair and took in the room.

Tess nervously followed his gaze. No one was looking at them, yet she didn't want to repeat it. Cade raised an eyebrow expectantly.

She sucked in a breath. "You have...good strategic thinking," she stated more firmly.

Cade grinned and took a sip of his water. Tess rolled her eyes and sipped her own.

"You look beautiful in that dress."

Tess almost choked on the water as she felt her face flush. She recovered her breath and tried to keep her tone mild. "Well, that's lame. It has nothing to do with DuskCabins."

"And you're funny," he added.

Now, she was really at a loss. She set her gaze back around the room and spotted the waiter returning with their food. Saved by the bell.

"Here comes our food," Tess said, returning her gaze forward.

She wondered if Cade would be disappointed that she wasn't flirting back the same way. It was so hard for her to be candid with her feelings. Instead, he just looked entertained, like he enjoyed the challenge. Maybe he preferred things this way.

As they ate, their conversation returned to the tournament and plans for training tomorrow. Then it moved to home and their families, but Tess began to realize the conversation constantly circled back to her. Her home. Her family. She wanted to know about Cade. What was his home like? Who was his family?

She set her fork down mid-story and blurted, "What about you?"

"What do you mean?" He raised an eyebrow.

"Tell me something about your home, your job, your childhood, your *anything*." She twirled her fork in the spaghetti as she spoke, trying not to push him too hard but unable to hold back any longer.

He sighed. "Growing up for me wasn't all rainbows and butterflies. I grew up in a rough part of San Diego. There was a lot of fighting at my school, and sometimes I was involved. Drugs, alcohol, parties…I used to think it was all so fun, but I've been trying to leave that stuff in the past."

"Trying?" she echoed. Why would he use that word? He had never mentioned any parties or fights before.

His eyes shifted back to the restaurant's interior, and he motioned to the waiter for their check. Tess glanced down at her own food. She had been full for the past five minutes, just playing with the food. Cade had finished his.

He paid the bill, and the two of them headed back outside. The night had grown cooler, and goosebumps appeared on Tess's arm.

"Have you ever seen Times Square?" Cade asked.

"No," Tess responded. "This is my first time in New York."

"It's only a few blocks from here."

She reached for his hand this time, and he led her through the city. After spending more time together, his touch was becoming familiar. As they moved through the crowds, Cade pulled her close and kept his arm between her and the other pedestrians. It felt nice to have someone looking out for her. Eventually, the noise grew louder. The streets brightened until they were surrounded by life and color on a block illuminated by big screens.

Tess spun in a circle, absorbing the entire setting. Every color from the rainbow and all the ones in between had to be on this block. Her eyes settled back on Cade, who watched her with a massive grin. His eyes widened, and he pointed past her toward the top of one of the buildings.

"Tess, look!"

She turned to see an advertisement for the Grand Championship. She smiled as it cycled through the games they were hosting and landed on DuskCabins. Suddenly, it scrolled through some of the qualifiers. Cade's face lit the big screen and then her very own.

"That's us!" Cade exclaimed.

She didn't respond. The moment felt surreal; it was hard to believe where she was. Two months ago, she had been in the hospital, unsure of what any future held for her, and now she was on a big screen in New York. And she was here with Cade.

She looked up at him and saw that he was already staring back down at her. Despite her instinct, she held onto his gaze this time. He leaned toward her, and she mirrored the movement until their lips met.

The feeling was both soft and electric, just like the lighting and rain. For a moment, it felt like they were the only two people in New York. For a moment, she forgot they were even in New York, but she was quickly reminded of this as an angry pedestrian bumped into her side.

Tess and Cade broke apart, and he grinned sheepishly at her.

"Get a room!" The pedestrian yelled.

She glanced back to Cade with a smirk. They already had two of those.

Chapter Seventeen
Preparing for Battle

Tess's alarm rang in the morning, startling her from her slumber. She glanced to the other side of her bed and saw Cade was no longer there. Visions of the previous night flashed through her mind: his hand in her hair, his tanned, muscular arms holding her body on top of his.

"Is this okay?" he had asked.

When she whispered a soft yes, he had tugged down her silk dress, his lips tracing her collarbone. She touched the spot where his lips had been and slumped back into the bed, hugging a pillow.

It stung slightly that he was already gone, but it wouldn't be too long before she was face-to-face with him again. Tess shook away the visions of the rest of the night and stood up from the bed suddenly. In thirty minutes, they needed to leave for the practice arena.

Crossing the room, she stepped over her discarded silk dress and knelt by her suitcase. She frowned as she realized in the craziness of last night, she had not taken her medication. She shrugged it off. She still felt fine. She moved to the shower and continued with her morning routine.

Another moment flashed through her mind: the feeling of Cade's bare body above her own. She shook her head again, trying to dismiss the thoughts. Was it going to be awkward to see Cade again after last night? She expected something might happen between them, but things had escalated quicker than she imagined. Still, she felt more excitement than worry.

Tara was right when she said it would come back to her, and the chemistry with Cade was so natural. It just felt right. Today, they would be busy, and she hoped this would not distract from the competition.

Once ready, she made her way to the lobby and spotted Cade laughing with a hotel staff member. His grin widened when he saw her approaching. She felt herself smiling back without even knowing what they were joking about.

"Here she comes! This is my partner, Tess." Cade touched Tess's shoulder as she arrived at his side. The front-end employee's eyes widened, but he masked that initial shock with a polite smile and nodded at Tess.

"Brian was just telling me that he's been playing DuskCabins for a year with some of his buddies," Cade explained. "They're all watching the tournament tomorrow."

"That's awesome!" Tess said, then she glanced back at Cade, unsure of how to keep the conversation moving.

He picked it back up easily. "I think we're both a little nervous but excited nonetheless! Anyway, we've got to head over for practice, Brian. I guess we will see you around." Cade nodded goodbye and then walked toward the exit. Tess followed closely behind as he called a taxi from his phone. In a few minutes they were on their way to the arena

"Sleep well?" Cade asked with a smirk from the passenger seat.

"Well enough." Tess faked a yawn, and Cade looked startled for a moment. She smiled deviously. "I'm kidding, relax."

There was a high in getting Cade flustered. But as their taxi approached a giant tournament arena, she knew she would have to ask him to return the favor very soon.

"Tess telling me to relax...how the tables have turned."

Adrian stood outside, next to a large, gated entrance, and waved when she noticed Tess and Cade approaching. Behind the gate, hundreds of fans milled around the elongated entrance, where various DuskCabins-themed games were set up, among other carnival-type games and vendor stalls.

There was merchandise being sold, and Tess was shocked to see her face on a T-shirt. It was the picture she'd submitted to SpersaGames. She grimaced. Maybe she should have spent more time choosing that photo.

"Great to see you guys!" Adrian began walking toward them. "Follow me toward the back before you're recognized. We're not doing fan time until later."

She wore a collared SpersaGames polo and brown khakis. Attached to a chunky belt was a black walkie-talkie that buzzed with static on and off. They walked past various security guards who didn't give them so much as a second glance with Adrian at the head.

"How was your night?" she asked. "Did you get to see much of New York City?"

Tess's mind could only go to one part of the night, so she was relieved when Cade quickly responded. "We made it to Times Square, and we saw ourselves on one of the big screens. They were advertising the tournament."

"Wow, I'm glad you guys caught it!"

They reached the back entrance to the building with a printed sign above the door reading 'Training Facilities'. Adrian scanned her badge, and Tess and Cade quickly followed her. The door closed behind them with a thunk as they stepped into a long hallway.

At the end was a folded table with ID badges similar to what Adrian wore sprawled across the top, with video game usernames and room numbers listed on them. Adrian hovered her hand over the ID badges, slowly scanning for JustATesst and BlackLantern, then handed them over to Tess and Cade.

"The way the training rooms are set up, you will not be placed with anyone else competing in DuskCabins. They are, however, limited, and you will be sharing a space with some competitors for another game," Adrian explained. "You'll be in room twenty-seven. Follow me."

They followed her to the left of the table, down another
lengthy hallway until pausing at room twenty-seven. Along the
way, they passed multiple players in uniform. Tess's mind told her
that there was no way she was supposed to be back here, but the
badge hanging from her neck reminded her that she belonged
here now.

Room twenty-seven was a small area with about ten
computers inside. On the left, five guys were practicing a MOBA
game, calling out plays. On the right, two computers sat side by
side, with their usernames labeled on small cards in front.

"You can practice here anytime you're free. We will have
lunch with all the DuskCabins participants at twelve, so I will
come back for you guys beforehand. Other than that, you both
have my number, so feel free to reach out if you need me." She
smiled and then quickly marched back out of the room—no
doubt to help out other participants.

"Ready to get your head back in the game?" Cade grinned as
he sat and launched DuskCabins.

Tess did the same, slipping into the seat beside him. She was
left speechless by the entire environment. It felt unreal. She had
difficulty grasping that this PC station had been prepared for her,
let alone the badge made for her.

A few of the other players glanced their way briefly but
returned to their game shortly after. Tess had never played that
game and could easily zone out their chatter. When she heard the
startup music of DuskCabins leaking through the headset in her
station, she remembered she would be able to escape to her own
little world soon enough.

"It's a little overwhelming," she finally admitted, adjusting
the headset over her carefully groomed hair.

"It is," Cade agreed. "But think of it like any other time
we've played." He put on his own headset, and their voices were
once again connected through the game, though they sat directly
next to each other.

"Do you want to start with one-v-ones?" Tess asked
mischievously.

It was the mode in which they fought each other. When Cade didn't immediately respond, she glanced over to see he was eying her with a sly grin and amused eyes.

"What?" she laughed. "You need the building practice."

"Alright, alright," he said, "Whatever helps you get comfortable."

They practiced against each other for the first hour. Unsurprisingly, Tess won most of the fights where they faced each other directly. Still, Cade had improved since they started practicing aggressive gameplay against each other, and that would be good for the tournament.

They switched it up shortly after, dropping into real matches and forcing their aggression against enemy players instead. Tess felt a bit rusty after just one day off for travel, so she was relieved that they had some time to practice before competing.

She would almost forget that Cade was next to her as they played, so lost in the world of the game, but when one of them died they would give the other a look. She would be reminded, that he was very much next to her and one glimpse of him would bring last night rushing back to the surface.

"Don't look at me like that, Tess."

She startled, wondering if he would bring it up in the middle of the arena. She thought it was clear what happened last night would go unspoken as they focused on the tournament instead.

"Like what?" She blinked innocently.

"Like I should have seen those kids coming from Newtown Square. I already know it's a popular spot to rotate from."

She relaxed but also felt disappointed. The unspoken rule was intact, but did last night mean to Cade what it meant to her?

Cade raised an eyebrow. "Well, am I right? Is that what you were thinking?"

She let the doubt fade, smiling. That was what she was thinking until she looked over at him. "It's alright. I'll finish this one out alone."

She turned back to the screen. There were six players left. Alone now, she stuck to the outskirts and rotated carefully. Cade minimized his own game, hovering his mouse over the time. "Adrian should be back after this match."

Cheers erupted across the room from the MOBA players, but Tess barely took note as she zoned in on finishing the game. She took down the rest of the competitors one by one, only struggling to fight the last player. Cade spectated from his own screen and called out some shots. Tess was reminded why she loved playing in a duo. Even if the other player was down, it was nice to have a second pair of eyes watching over things.

Shortly after her victory, Adrian came to collect them. They followed her through more hallways until they reached a large banquet room. The room was lined with tall bar-style tables, with white tablecloths dropped on top. On the left, there was a buffet-style array of chicken, vegetables, and fruit, the fresh aroma drifting toward the entrance. Competitors moved freely about, grabbing food and chatting.

Tess noticed EFN Perktuns standing across the room from the corner of her eye. She glanced back to Cade, who had followed her gaze and was already rolling his eyes.

He leaned toward her. "Your boyfriend's here," Cade breathed the comment so close to her ear that she could smell his mint gum.

She startled at the proximity and felt a chill run through her spine.

"Quiet," she hissed, shoving him gently and walking toward the buffet.

They both collected a dish and found a spot at an empty table in the center of the room. Shortly after, they were joined by another duo—two men who looked to be in their mid-twenties.

"I'm Daryn," the first said with a smile, nodding to Tess and then Cade. "And this is my duo, Nick."

"Nice to meet you, Daryn," Cade replied while Tess, midchew, waved. "My name's Cade, and this is Tess, my..." Her heart pounded as he hesitated to finish the sentence. Had she imagined the pause? "...duo."

"Is this your first tournament together?" Nick asked.

"Our first in-person," Cade answered.

"We've played plenty together online," Tess added after swallowing her bite.

"Well, this is a hell of a tournament for your first in-person," Daryn said with a laugh. He scratched his head and smiled at his partner, who nodded in agreement.

"What about you guys? Have you competed together long?" Tess asked. She leaned in toward the table, eager to learn more.

Nick glanced at Daryn before responding. "We've played together in some other tournaments for a few years now. Of course, DuskCabins is pretty new, so it will be our first time competing for this one."

"That's awesome! It must help to be comfortable playing together already," Cade said.

Tess glanced around the room. All the duos seemed pretty comfortable with their partners. She wondered if any were as fresh as her and Cade.

"You guys are sort of the new kids on the block," Daryn said, following her gaze. "A lot of these people are on teams or have been in other competitions together."

"I recognize some of them from Twitch," Tess said.

Nick nodded. "Yes, there's a lot of streamers here. Probably more than you recognize. Even though SpersaGames made it possible for anyone to get into this tournament, it's still dominated by a lot of the same faces."

"Well, it's a good thing we don't stand out too much already," Cade said dryly, motioning to Tess as he spoke.

She stuck out her tongue at him but laughed nervously afterward. She felt a lot of eyes on her, and the media definitely enjoyed focusing on her.

"I'm excited to see a girl in the tournament," Nick quickly added. He paused for a moment afterward and winced. "Not to single you out or anything."

Tess waved off his comment. "You wouldn't be the first."

"Well, my sister told me she's no longer rooting for my team." Daryn cut in to lighten the mood. "So, I have some issues."

Tess laughed, and the conversation returned to the game as they finished their food.

"I'm gonna grab seconds," Cade said, standing with his empty plate and heading back to the buffet.

"How'd you get into playing DuskCabins in the first place?" Nick asked.

"My brother and a few friends from home played it, so I just tried it out. I got really into solos and played all the time alone, but didn't realize the potential I'd hit until I duo'd with Cade." She glanced toward the buffet where Cade stood chatting with another pair of guys. They looked closer to her age.

"Your duo's talking to trouble one and trouble two over there," Daryn said in a hushed tone. Nick glanced over and nodded slowly.

"They're hard competition?" Tess squinted her eyes at them. The two guys were wearing matching navy-blue Esports jerseys.

"More like spoiled brats," Daryn said. "They've been on GSN for a while now, and they're notorious for getting in trouble with parties, drugs—stuff that gets you kicked if you're not careful."

"But wouldn't they be careful with what's at stake here?" Tess had been exposed to all that at college but avoided it for the most part. Especially now, after experiencing mania. She knew what it was like to slip away from yourself, and it bothered her that people chose to do it. Maybe she was jealous. It felt like she never got a choice when she lost control; it happened without instigation. She pushed back the thought of her mania before that became an issue again.

"I'm sure they'll be careful with the prize pool size in this competition, but they're bad news nonetheless."

Tess frowned as she watched how comfortably Cade laughed with the two guys. She turned back to her food. She would have to trust him, but that didn't stop the feeling of unease.

"I loved the replay of the ending of your qualifiers game," a new voice said. It belonged to a ginger man in a green Esports jersey. Beside him stood a teenage-looking boy with the same ginger hair and a matching shirt. Although there were few, she had noticed some younger competitors.

"Thanks, I owe that idea to Cade," she said as he returned to her side.

"Ahh, yeah, that was a fun one," Cade added, dropping his plate onto the table. "What's your name?"

"I'm Jackson, and this is my younger brother, Harry. He's my duo and a pain in my neck." He ruffled Harry's hair, earning him a silent glare from the freckled boy.

"Sounds like Tess," Cade joked. He reached out his hand to pretend to rustle her hair. She shot him one look, and he slowly lowered it.

Her plate was emptied now, and she glanced at the buffet. The scent carried over to where they stood now. She had a lot of socializing to do for the rest of the day and would need the energy.

"I'm gonna grab seconds," she said, picking up her plate. "Nice to meet you." She smiled carefully before turning to make her way across the room.

Cade easily picked up the conversation as she left. She hoped Cade would be with her for the meet-and-greets. Even those five minutes when he was gone felt a bit draining.

At the start of the line, Tess scooped more chicken onto her plate, followed by fruit and celery. A staff member placed a new heaping of mac and cheese into a tray standing on the table, and the smell overwhelmed her senses. She added some to her plate.

The duo Daryn had warned her about still stood toward the end of the buffet line, and she tried to avoid eye contact as she made her way out.

"Oi, gamer girl!" one of them called.

Tess froze. She turned slowly to face the two guys. One of them was sheepishly grinning, while the other was scanning her body up and down in a way that made her want to head back home for her baggy sweatpants and t-shirt.

"My name's Tess."

The one scanning her body snapped to attention and met her gaze.

"I'm Danny. This is my boy, Zach. Listen, we're having a little after-hours get-together later if you want to come by."

"Thanks for the offer, but I think I will concentrate on getting good sleep for the tournament tomorrow," she said shortly, then turned and began walking back toward Cade.

"Honey, you're gonna miss out! Your boy is making it all possible!" Danny called.

They were laughing, but she just kept walking and shook her head. She had no idea what they were talking about, but she would ensure that Cade respected getting as much rest tonight as she was.

"Try to ignore those idiots," another voice stopped her in her tracks. It was one she recognized immediately, even if it sounded a little different in person than over her computer speakers: EFN Perktuns.

He wore his iconic sky-blue jersey, and his perfect curly blonde hair framed his green eyes. His partner was missing, but she hardly recognized the duo he was competing with. She hadn't seen them compete too much together, but she knew he was on EFN as well.

"There's bound to be some in a group this big," she muttered, glancing back at Cade, who was still lost in conversation with Jackson and Harry. He crouched down to Harry's level and whispered something that made everyone laugh. She couldn't help but smile as she looked back to Perktuns.

"I'm Drew," he said, offering his hand. She realized she had not known his real name as she shook it. "And you're Tess."

Her eyebrows rose. Even if people had heard of her before this lunch, no one had been bold enough to drop her name.

"I've enjoyed your stream in the past," Tess admitted, encouraged by Drew's boldness.

He scratched the back of his neck and smiled. "You've seen it?"

"I think anyone that's used Twitch has seen it." Tess laughed.

"I don't want to say too much, but EFN is recruiting, and they've been looking for a girl that plays DuskCabins."

Tess stared back at him. Could he possibly be suggesting they were considering her? Before she could ask, he gestured to her plate. "Better finish eating. Meet and greets are starting soon."

She turned, dazed, and made her way back to the table. Jackson and Harry had moved on to talk to other competitors, but Nick and Daryn remained at the table. Cade glanced up as she approached, and he made a show of watching Drew walk the other way, using his hands as binoculars.

"You didn't faint?" he asked. He touched her forehead as if checking her temperature. She tried to ignore the spark she felt at his touch as she placed her plate down and then batted his hand away.

"Why would I faint? Drew and I are great friends," she said in a proper accent.

"Drew! Look at that! First name basis." He put his hand up for a high-five, but Tess rolled her eyes and returned her gaze to the table. In the distance, she watched Danny and Zach load up their plates again.

She took a deep breath. "Cade...you're planning on getting plenty of rest tonight, right?"

"If you let me," Cade replied a little too quickly.

Daryn and Nick gave each other a look, and Tess cursed Cade for opening his arrogant mouth. He seemed to regret it, too, as he took in Tess's angry stare.

"That's not what I meant—" she began but was cut off by surprise when a hand was placed on her shoulder and Cade's.

They spun around to see Adrian beaming. "We've got to get you guys moving for the meet-and-greet!"

Tess glanced around the room to see that the other duos were being moved as well. She shoved one last bite of mac and cheese into her mouth and followed Adrian out of the room, feeling unsure about Cade's response.

Chapter Eighteen
Wake-Up Call

Tess woke up half an hour before her alarm was supposed to go off on the tournament day. The prior day had been exhausting, though it was rewarding to meet so many people who were rooting for her in this tournament. After meet and greets, she and Cade had explored the city more. He made good on his offer to find them some hotdogs.

Tess asked that they leave what was going on between them for after the tournament, so he didn't come back to her room last night. She hoped they could focus on getting more rest and revisit what was happening between them soon after.

Moving to the half-emptied gift basket SpersaGames left for her, Tess pulled out her jersey from the bottom. It was light violet in color and made of slick material. Golden calligraphy sprawled across the front, stating "Grand Championship." Her username was in a plain white font across the back. She took a deep breath. It was hard to believe the day had finally come.

She glanced at her medications on the bathroom sink and frowned.

"I'm going back as soon as this is over," she whispered. If playing in a duo had taught her anything, it was that she could open up to people. There were people she could depend on, even if it sometimes felt uncomfortable.

A knock at the door made her jolt.

She moved the medications to her suitcase, threw on the jersey, and opened the door. Adrian was on the other side, and beside her was a stout man in a police uniform. Tess frowned. Was she going to need an escort today? She hadn't thought it would be that crazy at the arena. Adrian wasn't looking at Tess; instead, her eyes focused on the officer.

"Tess Caulbaugh?" he asked.

Tess stiffened at the harsh tone. "Yes?"

"Is it okay if I quickly sweep your room?" He gestured inside.

"Yes," she said slowly. She gave a bewildered look to Adrian, who had yet to meet her gaze, and then stepped back to allow the two to enter the room.

Adrian hugged the wall while the officer carefully walked through her gift basket, dresser drawers, and suitcase. Tess opened her mouth a few times but was so caught off guard that she could hardly conjure a sentence. He paused while examining her pills.

"They're prescription," she said.

"I see," the police officer responded. His eyes squinted at the label, but he seemed satisfied and dropped them back down. He walked across the room and stood next to Adrian. "Her room's clear," he said.

Tess raised an eyebrow at Adrian, who nervously smoothed her skirt and said, "Tess, Cade has been disqualified from the competition due to possession of illegal drugs."

Tess's heart stopped. She couldn't believe it. She wouldn't believe it. And yet a uniformed police officer was standing right before her, nodding. She blinked as if he would magically disappear. Still there.

She stepped back, and her vision became a little blurry. Was it blurry because she was overwhelmed or because of the warm droplets that began to fill her eyes? She blinked a few more times, and they began to cascade down her cheeks. She might have felt self-conscious about it in another moment, but right now, she barely registered that they were there.

"What?" she asked. It was all she could muster.

"You are still eligible to compete as a solo competitor against the other duos, but Officer Ramirez would like to ask you a few questions." Adrian's voice was shaky yet firm.

Tess wondered if this was something that had ever happened before. She stepped back another time and gripped the edge of the bed.

"Tess, how long have you known Cade?" the officer asked as he flipped out a small notebook and pen.

"Just for the past few months," she answered.

Did she know Cade?

He scribbled down a note, then returned his gaze to her. "Did he ever mention his work to you? What does he do outside of the game?"

He asked the question as if there was no doubt that this topic would have surfaced in the time they'd known each other. Tess suddenly felt embarrassed for how little she knew. It had worked well for her because she didn't have to share what she did outside the game.

"No—I...I guess we just focused on the game."

He simply nodded and continued writing notes. "Have you been to his room at the hotel here?"

"No," Tess answered quickly, then glanced at Adrian. Did she really need to get into what transpired between them? "...he's only been to this one." She thought about the two of them lying on her bed, then her stomach twisted. Her hand touching the comforter felt numb, and she pushed her weight back off it, standing shakily in the center of the room.

"Has he ever mentioned being on drugs? Or offered you any? Cocaine?"

"No...never. He's never mentioned anything about drugs to me. I've been with him almost this entire weekend. I didn't think he was..."

She thought about his endless energy. The way he refused to open up about his life back home. His friend had joined the voice call. What had he called him? Snow White. But wouldn't she have known if he was high? She had never been around anyone on cocaine, but she felt like it would be something you would have noticed.

"Have you been in contact with the competitors, Danny Melnin or Zach Bracho?"

"I met them for the first time at lunch yesterday."

They had mentioned a party. They were the ones who were supposed to be in trouble. Not Cade. She blinked back more tears. How could she do this without Cade? How could Cade do this to her?

"They reported Cade as a dealer, and we found the drugs in his room. He was taken into custody last night."

Tess glanced back to Adrian, who was nodding sympathetically. "You can talk to him before the tournament, but you will compete alone." She stepped a little closer and smiled sadly. "There are a lot of people looking forward to seeing you play, Tess. I know this must be incredibly disappointing, but don't let it drag you too far down. I've seen clips of what you can do even when you're the only player still alive."

She seemed to be waiting for a response, but all Tess could do was stand there and try to process the news. After a few seconds, Adrian and the officer gave a short goodbye and exited the room. Tess collapsed back on top of the bed and stared at the ceiling.

She had felt so sure that she knew Cade, and she had felt such a strong connection to him. He didn't know all her problems, and she didn't know all his, but that had been fine until now. She grabbed the pillow where his head had rested just two days prior and threw it across the room with a grunt.

Of all things, drugs? She had been running so intently toward feeling like herself, feeling stable again. And he was over there perfectly healthy already and just tossing it away. She felt like she didn't know him at all. She was certain she didn't know him at all.

She'd worried that meeting in person might complicate things, but their chemistry remained. She knew from that first touch the soft rain and the lightning. She had worried about the thunder, but she had somehow deluded herself into believing that it wouldn't come, that they were special, different. She had to smile at her own stupidity. How could she still be so stupidly optimistic after everything she had been through?

She thought about the long nights spent playing together, the times they just sat in the lobby and talked about anything, the texts, the teasing, and the way he remembered small things, like her meal preferences. She gave up therapy for their team, and all the while, he was partying it up, making more money on the side. Were the tournaments not enough?

Then again, that wasn't entirely true. She hadn't quit therapy for Cade. She gave it up for the tournament and also because she didn't want to deal with the trauma. He hadn't even known she was in therapy. He had never asked her to stop. He didn't owe her anything.

She tried to believe that, but she still felt he owed her.

He was the one who found her. He was the one that insisted on competing. He was the only one who saw her outside of her breakdown when no one else could. But it was the games that gave her this second chance. It was her skill that got her to this tournament. She told her mom that her recovery was separate from Cade, and she wanted to believe that was true. She wanted to believe she could do this thing without Cade.

She walked to the mirror and wiped the tears from her face. Her black eyeliner was smudged across her face like a warrior paint. She washed away the makeup and patiently redid it. She would not be wasting any more time on tears. She reconsidered. She would not be wasting any more time on tears until after the tournament.

She took out her phone and numbly blocked Cade's number. She did not care if she was allowed to speak to him before the tournament. He'd done enough to ruin the day. She took a deep breath and walked out of her room. She would need all the practice she could get this morning, and she could not wait to get in a game and wreak havoc.

Chapter Nineteen
The Grand Championship

Tess followed Adrian out of the small training room and through winding hallways inside the tournament arena. She'd spent the morning aggressively dropping in as a solo player against duos and pushing the thought of Cade far away. Locked away with the mania.

When she first sat down for practice, she felt the emptiness of the PC station beside her. He had just been sitting there and practicing with her yesterday. But, once she was in a game, the idea of Cade would fade. It was just her and one goal: winning.

Adrian didn't mention Cade when she arrived to retrieve Tess. She only grinned and told her it was time.

As they walked, Tess recalled yesterday's meet and greets— the number of people she had rooting for her that she didn't even know. Beyond that, she had friends and family who would watch from home. There were the kids she had met at the airport, and her face was displayed on the big screen in Times Square.

It had been followed by Cade's but presented separately. Her face faltered momentarily as she thought of how the press presented them together. She knew there would be questions after he was absent today. She knew it would draw even more attention to herself.

Not only was she the stand-out girl, but now she was the stand-out lost-her-duo-to-drug-possession girl. She smiled sickly at that title. To think she had been so worried about being labeled as the bipolar girl, it never occurred to her there could be other labels to look out for.

Although, she supposed the lost-her-duo-to-drug-possession girl title was better than the lost-her-duo-to-drug-possession-and-coping-with-bipolar girl title. At least she got to keep something to herself.

"Alright, it's just up these stairs," Adrian said, pulling Tess out of her spiral.

Tess found herself lining up behind other competitors with Adrian at her side. She kept her gaze low. She didn't want to see Danny or Zach's smug expressions or catch any confused looks when the other duos began to notice Cade was missing.

As she approached the top of the steps, sound hit her like a wave. A roaring crowd and DuskCabins music being DJ'd against popular tracks. She hadn't known what exactly to expect, but she hadn't anticipated the crowd would be large enough to emit this noise level.

She followed the other players into the center of a square structure in the arena. It was lined with PCs sitting side by side against half-walls, forming a cube that rose in the middle of a large audience.

The top half of the wall was open, revealing a view of the audience that surrounded the square arena, with seats traveling far toward the ceiling. There were large screens all around the room, and blue and white lights flashed, dancing across the crowd in strobe patterns.

Adrian pointed her toward a station on the lower level. Her chair was labeled with her gamertag. Tess approached it slowly and took her seat.

Announcers sounded over the music, calming the audience, but the words were muffled to Tess as she lifted on the heavy headset that was waiting for her. Adrian gave her a thumbs-up and left the arena. Tess watched her go, but at the sight of other players, she quickly turned back toward her screen. In the upper corner, there was a timer ticking down from thirty. Below the timer, it said 'Game 1/3'.

Tess took a few more breaths.

"Just like any other tournament," she reminded herself.

The timer ticked down slowly until the screen faded to a start.

Tess watched player after player fly off the side of the plane before she decided to descend herself. She wanted to start on the outskirts of the map because there was no way she would survive without a duo in Metropolis, not against the players in this tournament.

She braced for a landing and rolled softly onto the farmlands, where loot was scattered alongside wheat. She watched another duo parachute toward a small town to her left and two more to the right within the same village.

Wheat crunched beneath her feet as she sprinted across the field for loot. She had to move quickly if she was going to make up for being solo. Much to her luck, along the way she picked up a rare shotgun, chest armor, and a standard assault rifle. It was the loadout she moved most confidently with, and it felt right that RNG—the random decider of where items would spawn—would at least be on her side if her duo wouldn't.

She wasted no time moving toward the small town where she had watched the other two duos land but traveled cautiously, stopping behind structures occasionally to check her back while she was covered. She bet that no one would expect a threat approaching from the farmlands. There wasn't enough loot for two players to drop there at the start.

Steps sounded in a red brick home within the town. Tess busted through the front door, banking on the element of surprise. Inside, a ninja stood in the center of the room, gathering ammo sprawled across the carpet.

He spun to fight, but Tess brought him down with one shot. He attempted to crawl over to the exit in his knocked state, but she finished him off with another. The only loot to spill from his body was a common pistol. Useless. She ran right past it for the exit.

There was no doubt his partner would want revenge, and now they knew she was here.

Without pausing outside, she built ramps to reach the roof and made protection around her body, covering every angle. She patiently waited for the teammate to come to investigate, which he did through a sniper shot that rang above her head.

Tess narrowed her eyes. She wondered if he had also noted the second team that landed across town. Perhaps she had only been able to tell from her position at the farmlands, and he was unaware. His boldness in the ranged shot led her to believe that was the case.

Assault rifle shots erupted from the other end of town. They were targeting the sniper. Letting the battle play out would be safer, but Tess wouldn't have time for this type of break between eliminations. Every kill counted.

She jumped out, away from her own protection, and sprinted across town toward the sound of the assault rifles.

The other duo stood confidently under a water tower, focused on the sniper who was frantically building protection over and over again on the roof of a barn. They continued to spray down his cover from both angles faster than he could rebuild it. He was taking some damage, but not enough.

Tess pulled out her assault rifle and killed both of the players on the street. She began building her own platforms toward the barn without stopping to examine their loot.

She was sure the remaining player had to have low health, and she didn't want to give him time to heal. She could make out the sound of ripping bandages as she neared his cover. He was trying to heal, but it wouldn't matter; he didn't have much more time.

As soon as her ramp connected with the roof, the player dropped the bandages and broke down his wall to take a shot at Tess. She attempted to dodge the shot, but it scraped past her arm, taking a quarter of her health with it.

Tess swore and took her own shot. Her opponent threw up another wall in front of him before it could connect. He was a peek-a-boo type of player. Cade would have wanted to take him on from a distance, but he was not here. She grimaced and took her shotgun back out, then continued to push toward him.

When he dropped his wall to take another shot, she anticipated it and put up her own wall to block it, mirroring his strategy. Suddenly, there was a clicking sound. He had to be reloading. This was her chance. She built right up above his post.

On top of the small fort, she began to spray shots through the ceiling. He sprayed his own rifle straight up desperately, but she continued to wait for the moments when he would have to reload to unload her own. Eventually the timing came together, and she was able to connect a few shots. It seemed the bandages hadn't healed him that well because when her shots connected, he instantly vanished.

Tess felt the floor shake as the audience roared outside her tiny DuskCabins world. The big screens must have been displaying their battle. She tried to ignore the noise as she sifted through the loot he left behind. He had a rare sniper rifle and some leftover bandages. She wrapped them around her own arm as she caught her breath.

An alarm sounded in the distance, indicating that the zone would be closing in. Tess examined her map and saw the circle was closing in on the northeast side of the map. She had a journey ahead of her coming from the farmlands, but that would be good because other players would be pushing in as well. More opportunities for attack.

She targeted the factories as her next destination and dropped from the barn roof. Neglecting the dirt trail connecting the two areas, she opted to continue through the woods instead. She would be covered better that way. As she pushed along, she encountered three more duos. Each resulted in an intense build battle, which she barely survived. Luckily, every duo left enough bandages and shields behind to regain full armor and health.

Tess was so lost in the game and so satisfied with it being that way. She felt the emotion and anger toward Cade fueling every motion she made.

Finally, as the zone closed, she found herself on a cliff overlooking the factories. Two duos were battling out on the top of the central roof, and despite her natural instinct, she stayed put. They had the high ground, and she'd learned from her three build fights, as expected, that these players were no joke.

Another duo appeared on a neighboring rooftop, taking shots at the two teams already facing off. Tess pulled out the rare sniper rifle she had looted from the elimination at the barn. She focused the scope on one of the new players standing atop the second factory building and easily knocked him. His teammate quickly moved to build a cover for both of them, but one of the players in the central fight finished her kill and then took the other.

"Shit."

She had wanted both of those kills, but without support, charging in for them would have been suicide. She moved the scope across an alley and aimed for the main roof, where the player who had taken her kills stood. She released a shot that knocked him to the ground. His partner was tied up in the ensuing fight, and she was able to take another shot to finish him off.

She moved the scope toward the partner but paused at the sound of construction behind her. Tess dropped the sniper rifle and turned, defensively raising her arms to bring walls around her at every angle.

There were ten players left, and she had likely made her spot well-known from all the sniper rifle shots. Shots slammed into her cover from both sides.

"Shit," she murmured. She repeatedly rebuilt the cover, but she knew it was hopeless. Eventually, her walls crumbled faster than she could rebuild them, and she was completely exposed to her opponents. They killed her easily.

She heard the audience "Ohhh" eerily in sync, and a score of twelve was displayed on her screen. Her body untensed. That had to be a high score here. Sure, she and Cade had pulled off scores in the twenty range, but that had been against randoms. This was against elite duos.

She watched as the final players fought it out, and then the rankings appeared. Out of the fifty duos, Tess was in fourth place. She grinned and thought perhaps she could handle a Metropolis drop after all.

As Tess dropped from the plane this time, she followed about half the other players toward Metropolis. She aimed for a pizza shop on the southwest edge of town. One that she and Cade would normally target on a risky drop like this.

Gliding toward the roof, she noticed another duo seemingly aiming to land there as well. She quickly redirected herself to a neighboring apartment building, where she landed on a second-story balcony. As soon as her feet hit the concrete, she snatched up a common pistol and broke down the sliding door, climbing inside over shards of glass.

On top of a queen bed draped in a tapestry comforter was some common armor. It was not an ideal start, but she would have to make the most of it.

A thud echoed from the floor above. Another player had landed there.

Tess froze, listening for a second set of footsteps. It seemed to be just one player. Every part of her wanted to chase down this opponent and take him alone before his partner could show up. But she exercised patience and backed into the corner of the bedroom, crouching next to a wooden dresser, hoping to stay hidden until they passed.

This plan immediately backfired as the ceiling crumbled above Tess, plaster flying down. The player was breaking through the ceiling. Tess took a deep breath and fired four perfect pistol shots as the player dropped into the room. He was knocked prone on the ground. She finished the kill, but unfortunately, he didn't leave behind any new loot. She'd have to stick with the pistol.

Tess paused and listened again. There were footsteps on the bottom floor. Likely a partner seeking revenge. Crossing the hallway, Tess ducked into another apartment, closing the door softly behind her. There were four more units on the floor, and she didn't want it to be clear which one she was waiting in.

She didn't so much as switch guns to avoid making any noise from where she camped. She frowned at herself for the cowardly strategy; it was not her proudest, but she was working from whatever angle she could at this point.

Finally, footsteps sounded outside the door, and she took aim for where his head would be when it opened. He kicked open the door with his own gun ready—a rare assault rifle. Even with a close range, he was doing more damage with that gun than she could do with her pistol. Tess connected two shots before a clicking noise sounded, and she realized she would need a few seconds to reload.

Ducking through an open bedroom at half health, Tess reloaded her pistol, then slid back out toward the entrance. She fired three more shots into the kitchen. The moment was enough to throw off her opponent, and he died with her last shot. She let out a breath and collected the rifle, then listened for any more footsteps in the building. With only silence, Tess tore back out to search the rest of the building for loot.

In the lobby Tess discovered three healing potions. She gulped them down desperately, cool liquid splashing on her face, and then she listened again for noise. All she could hear was the faint buzzing of air conditioning units.

She climbed back up to the roof and scanned the streets. A few players darted between buildings. She brought up walls for cover and then took careful shots. She was able to bring down three players. It seemed like her opponents were hard at work finishing off those players' partners, as each contestant was killed instantly.

Firing sounded close from the east, and she realized she may have overstayed her welcome in this spot. It was time to keep moving. She exited back through the building's ground floor and prayed that she was moving discretely as she made her way closer to the gunfire. As she traveled deeper into the city, she passed a few desolate shops. There was a rustling in a bakery to her right. Maybe they weren't so desolate.

"Shit," she whispered.

She hoped to make it to the loud gunfire before encountering anyone else, and she had left herself pretty wide open for an attack. She ducked carefully into an alley and aimed her sight at the shop's entrance. It was a wooden door, already swung wide open.

A shot from above startled her from her position, and her health was cut in half. Her gaze snapped up to the roof, and she saw that a cheerleader had a rifle aimed down at her. Someone was covering their duo as they looted.

Tess quickly built a wall and a roof to cover her position. At the same time, the player that she had heard inside the shop rushed out the entrance, ready for combat.

Tess swapped out her rifle for the pistol and swiped her hand to bring down the wall in front of her; she took four rapid shots—leaving the player on the street low—but the cheerleader, who remained untouched on the roof, started firing down again.

Tess built desperately against their gunfire and tried to back further into the alley. She noted a rusty sewer that would provide an escape from the duo. It was going to be too hard to take them both down.

That's when she heard it. A shotgun blast. She stopped in her tracks at the sound. The player who was on the ground with her had a shotgun, and she wanted that gun. She took a breath and turned back toward the fight. She drew her pistol, crouched, and took another shot at the player in the street. He dropped to the ground instantly, knocked.

Tess desperately built cover above her so that she could finish the kill and grab the loot. All she wanted was the shotgun; she would just grab it and go.

Surprisingly, the shots weren't spraying down on her anymore. A bullet rang past her ear, and she quickly realized this was because the player on the roof had dropped down to her level. They stood behind her on the street now.

She popped the knocked player for the full kill, but it was taking too long. She was exposed for his duo, and he finished her off with his own shotgun. Without a partner, she died instantly. No chance for revival.

Tess tried to hide her disappointment. She knew that her face was being live streamed for any interested viewers, and she was sure at least a few people were watching. She had been greedy. She wanted that shotgun but didn't have cover, so she needed to remember that. She hadn't been to Metropolis alone in a very long time.

She spectated the rest of the match, reacting alongside the crowd, and her heart sank at all the kills she couldn't even try to obtain. Finally, the standings were rereleased, and out of all the duos, she had dropped to twenty-three. It wouldn't be a very lucrative tournament if she couldn't adapt to being solo for this last game.

She couldn't land at Metropolis, especially with no guarantee of finding a shotgun fast enough, but perhaps she could try something else. Somewhere with a view of the town. Unpopular like the farmlands, but more central to the map.

The audience cheered as the final match was announced, and Tess channeled all her emotions. She was a solo player before she met Cade, and that was how she learned to play the game. Of course, she hadn't played solo in matches against pro-level duos, but that was just a technicality.

She thought about how much anger she had for Danny and Zach for what they had done. Even if she felt confused and disappointed about Cade, it was only hatred for those two. They were somewhere in this match, and she could imagine every player was them until the entire lobby was cleared.

She wouldn't be greedy. She wouldn't land hot. She would work with what she found and remember she was alone in this. Most importantly, she would remember why she wanted to take everyone out.

Chapter Twenty
The Final Fight

This time, as half the lobby made their way toward Metropolis, Tess hung back on the plane. She dropped to a mountain top outside the city a few moments later. She was the only player to make the drop on the mountain, and she was not very surprised about that—the loot was limited.

Scattered between rocks, a few items were waiting for her: chest armor, bandages, and an uncommon sniper rifle. She grinned at the sight of the sniper rifle, snatched it up, and suddenly forgave the game for holding back on her shotgun in the last match.

Peering through the scope, she aimed toward Metropolis. At this distance, it was a mess of players building, running, and fighting. She carefully followed each fight with the gun and took shots when the opportunity presented itself.

The opportunity presented itself eleven times. Tess took ten kills from those shots. One player had been saved by his partner. At this distance, in a regular game more players were likely to be healed, but there were enough skilled opponents in the area to finish what she started. They were making quick work taking out the partners.

Finally, as the initial fighting slowed, Tess realized she would need to creep into the city. She had nothing to use in a close combat fight. She carefully dropped down the side of the mountain, placing platforms below her feet at tolerable distances to help break the fall. A few drops later, she rolled onto the grass and stood, sprinting for the left side of the city.

From her view on the mountain, she had only seen one surviving duo that stuck to the nightclub area on the right side of town. The zone closed as she moved, and Metropolis was at the center.

Inside the city, simply by walking through the streets, she came across a plethora of loot. She quickly gathered a normal assault rifle, a rare shotgun, and some grenades. She kept her sniper rifle and found a lot more ammo for it.

Once Tess was satisfied with the loot, she climbed to a rooftop vantage point and searched for the duo she'd spotted from the mountainside. They were still circling the southeast part of town, and she had the chance for a clear shot.

She scoped in the sniper rifle, but the moment that her crosshairs lined up with one of their heads, she paused and lowered it. Without Cade, she didn't have the cover she was used to, but if she were to keep the other duo alive, she did have two free distractions.

She stashed her gun away and moved carefully along the rooftops, staying low and quiet until she was closer to her opponents. She remained behind pre-existing cover and didn't build a single thing. She could not risk drawing attention to herself.

Her worst nightmare had come true; she would have to be patient.

Eventually, the duo seemed satisfied with their loot and moved out of Metropolis, heading for the far southeast side of the zone, assumingly headed for the lake house. Tess tailed them carefully while consistently glancing over her shoulder for other opponents. If she were to spot any, she wouldn't engage, or else she'd find herself sandwiched. Instead, she would reposition herself.

Halfway toward the lake house, the duo encountered another group, and a build battle unfolded. Tess ducked behind a nearby shed while structures were amassed in the woods before her. She waited, studying the duos to determine which pair would be harder to face. She judged how the players built and then took her shots.

It took three sniper shots to bring down the stronger pair, but she was able to take them both down. She had carefully timed the shots, striking only when the opponents were hidden from the other duo. That way, it was harder for the remaining duo to tell exactly which direction the sniper rifle shots had come from.

As the living duo emerged to the top of their structure, Tess again ducked behind the shed and listened. She frowned at the rustling from above as the duo stole the loot from her kills. The two players left alive weren't the group she had initially been following, but they seemed less skilled and, therefore, would be easier to kill at the end.

Clanking sounded as they dropped back down through the structure, eventually landing on the ground. She followed at a safe distance as they began to walk through the woods. They were heading north toward the factories.

Along the way, Tess spotted another duo heading toward Metropolis. The team she had spared didn't seem to notice, and she let out a frustrated breath. She threw a grenade at the pair heading toward Metropolis, then crouched behind a thick fallen log.

The recipients of her grenade quickly snapped their heads in her direction but looked right past her, locking eyes on the duo headed for the factories. They fired assault rifle shots at the factory duo, who then began to build.

As the fighting dragged on, Tess noticed that the factory duo seemed to be connecting more shots than the pair Tess had attracted with the grenade. She decided then that the factory's duo needed to be eliminated. She crawled on her stomach carefully through the woods until she had a clean shot. The factory duo had protected their bodies from the pair headed for Metropolis, but not from her.

She took back-to-back sniper rifle headshots, eliminating both of the players. Loot spilled from their bodies, and she had to forcefully tear her gaze away from the golden shotgun that sat in their place. Closing her eyes, she replayed the ending of the last match in her head. She would not make the same mistake.

She glanced back to the players she'd lured into the fight. They were building up a more defensive structure, anticipating a push from her, but she wouldn't be pushing. She crawled further from where she took her shots, past a patch of shadowed mushrooms, remaining low and out of sight.

Eventually, the other duo let up and moved in for the loot left behind by the players she had killed. They watched carefully for any sight of the sniper, but Tess didn't dare to move a muscle. She waited them out.

After looting, the group continued on their path toward the Metropolis. Tess allowed some distance to grow before tailing after them. The zone was closing in again. At the end of the match, it would be centered on Metropolis. There were seven other players left, and although Tess knew this was a high-kill game for her, she did not know how high her score needed to be to place.

The duo paused at a house outside of the city and began to construct a metal fort. Tess remained at a safe distance, crouched on a hill much like where she started, but at the opposite side of the Metropolis.

The sound of shots echoed across the city, and she scoped her sniper rifle in on the commotion. She got two more kills on two separate groups before the zone pushed in even tighter, and she was forced to enter the city.

The duo she had been following had also tried to get the kills; they had even done some of the damage for her, but she waited for the right times to strike, ensuring she was the one who had the last shot.

With four other players remaining, the duo Tess followed decided to press in on a gun down happening in the middle of town. It seemed the other two were not on the same team. Tess waited a few moments as the duo took some initial shots across the city, attempting to take out the other two players who were facing each other. Then Tess took her own shots at the gun down pair.

Suddenly, something clicked in the minds of the opponents she had been following, and they turned to face her. She had wondered when the other duo would finally investigate who was finishing all their kills.

Tess sprang into action, rapidly building platforms, and they both mirrored her actions. Across town, the other fight ended, and the remaining player began to take shots at the duo that built against her. Luckily, she was not the one sandwiched in the middle, and she intended to keep it that way.

Tess paused her building and looked down at the duo. She had just a few seconds to take shots before they would catch up to her, and she had to make them count. She sprayed down, damaging the opponents, but Tess cursed when there was no knock.

She shook her head and continued to build before they could return fire. A rocket sounded from the other side of the city, and Tess peered over her ramp. She was forced to watch the final opponent wipe out both players she had stalked so carefully in one breath.

Covering herself with a wall, Tess dropped down and picked up a gleaming golden shotgun sitting right where their bodies had disappeared. It was the same one the players had looted from the duo heading toward factories.

"I believe that belongs to me," she said.

Laughter sounded from a whole different world in the distance. Tess had completely forgotten that anyone else was listening in on the game.

She narrowed her eyes and rushed in for the last player. Her opponent was ready. He took shots with the rocket launcher as she closed in the distance. She brought up a wall at each shot, and it was immediately blown to bits.

Tess grinned. After all this waiting and stalking, she could finally go all in.

The player started building for a height advantage, and Tess did the same. She closed in tight until she blocked off every ramp he attempted to build. Now directly above him, she started spraying assault rifle shots onto his roof.

The roof also acted as her floor, so she dropped into the box with him when it finally shattered. He fired instantly, and anticipating this, Tess ducked low. The shot missed. Then she pulled out her golden shotgun.

One headshot ended the game.

"Victory this round goes to JUSTATESSST," a voice echoed in the distance.

She glanced at her monitor and realized it wasn't in the distance. It was in the stadium. She blinked in surprise as she adjusted back to the real world. The crowd was roaring again, and the standings appeared on her screen.

After the last game, with the number of kills she had dropped and the victory bonus she earned from the win, Tess had moved into tenth place. Ten out of fifty duos. 38 points as a solo player. It was not bad at all, she thought. She smiled genuinely despite everything. She had won $300,000.

She blinked again, and Adrian was by her side. She rushed her out of the arena and through the winding halls.

"The press is dying to speak with you," Adrian said.

Tess tried to formulate a response, but she still felt lost to the game. Noise seeped in from every direction. People pushed past her from every angle, and the emotion from the morning started crashing back to the surface.

Finally, Tess said, "I don't think that's a great idea."

"I don't blame you." Adrian glanced at her sympathetically.

A wave hit Tess. A wave that had formed early this morning and waited patiently as she competed before it crashed back down on her now.

She was beyond elated by her performance, but the weight of that happening without Cade started to sink in. The fact that she hadn't spoken to him yet, that she didn't even have the answers for what the press might be asking her. Crash. For what her friends would be asking her. Crash. The answers that she wanted to know. Crash. Did she want to know? Crash.

Her body ached, and her head begged for sleep. The medication still had an effect on her, and she wondered again if it was even necessary. She was clearly handling a lot on her own. She hadn't felt manic before that first instance in her life—at least not in that extreme way—and she hadn't felt manic again since. She was sick of the side effects and could clearly care for herself.

She didn't need the help from anyone or anything.

"Tess?"

A lanky woman stepped into their path. She wore a light pink business suit and had a backstage pass. Tess tried to muster a smile that said, 'I was not just contemplating the validity of my mental illness, nor was I upset over my drug dealer video game partner, but instead thinking about my epic victory'.

It was hard to say that with a smile, but the other woman seemed satisfied as she continued, "Congratulations on your victory. My name is Victoria Clark. I work for EFN. I won't bother you while you should be celebrating, but I wanted to give you my card and tell you to call tomorrow if you are interested in a position with us."

"Thank you, it's nice to meet you. I'm very interested." Tess had forgotten all about her conversation with Drew.

She took the card, and Victoria disappeared down the hallway. Adrian finished walking Tess back to the exit, where a taxi was waiting.

The ride back to the hotel was short. The driver smiled and asked her how the tournament had gone. He didn't know much about the game, and Tess didn't feel like bragging about the win, so some of the ride went by in silence.

She wished she had someone to celebrate this victory with. Someone who would understand everything that had just unfolded. Someone who would know exactly what to say. Okay, so she wished Cade was still there. How she could wish that after the decisions he'd made was beyond her.

"How do you feel?" the taxi driver asked as he dropped her off.

She had finally admitted to winning the last game.

"Great!" she called as she exited the taxi. The air had turned crisp.

The yellow car screeched right back onto the busy street.

"Alone," she whispered as she stood on the curb, watching it disappear. Light rain began to fall, splattering on the pavement.

As she entered the hotel, her phone buzzed with congratulations, missed calls, and, worst of all, questions about Cade. She turned it off.

She glanced at her pills, and her stomach twisted.

For once, she welcomed the dreamless exhaustion as she collapsed on the bed.

Chapter Twenty-One
Victory Celebrations

A couple of hours later, Tess woke up to find that the world outside had traded daylight for streetlights. She felt the fabric of her shirt to confirm that she was still wearing her Esports jersey and sat up at the sound of her stomach grumbling.

She groaned and rolled over to reach for the bedside table, where a room service menu sat next to the hotel phone. She skimmed through the options and tried to decide between pizza, a burger and fries, or wings, then remembered her victory—what the fuck—she ordered all three.

After calling in her order, Tess glanced around her room, looking for a way to pass the time while she waited for the food. Eventually, her gaze landed on her cell phone. It sat in the corner of the room on the desk, still powered off from earlier. Tess sighed. She knew she was going to have to face people sooner or later.

She made her way to the phone and pressed the power button. Text messages flooded in at rapid fire, the text tone dinging repeatedly. She fought the urge to turn it right back off.

Andrea: My best friend's a badass!
Andrea: What happened to your boo?
Jordan: Where the fuck was Cade?
Jordan: Congrats too! Lol
Tara: CONGRATS!

Tara: BTW...Do I need to hurt someone?
Mom: Darling, you did wonderful.
Mom: What happened to Cade?
Mom: Don't forget your meds in this craziness!
Mom: Call when you can, we love you!
Dad: Proud of your performance today! Your brother explained the game while we were watching.
Grandma: Good job on winning! Love you! Love, Grandma.

Finally, the messages stopped, and Tess stared at the screen, contemplating who she should call. She opened to her most recent texts with Cade. She wanted answers. She wanted to hear his voice.

"No, you don't," she told herself out loud.

She wasn't going to brush over what had happened this morning and wasn't ready to talk to him. She closed out of their chat and clicked into the group chat with her friends, starting a Facetime call with Andrea, Jordan, and Tara.

Andrea picked up first, still wearing business casual from her internship. "There she is!" she hollered.

Jordan and Tara popped in.

"Ms. Moneybags," Jordan added.

Tara just smiled and waited for Tess to speak.

"Hey, guys..." Tess didn't know where to start. She tried to think of a soft way to put what had happened.

"I watched the tournament with my brother. You were badass!" Jordan said.

"We all watched," Tara added. "I noticed the new shirt, and I adore it."

"What I noticed," Andrea started carefully, then backtracked. "...besides your amazing performance...was you were flying solo."

Tess dropped her gaze to the ground and then slowly returned it to her friends. They were waiting in careful anticipation. There was no simple way to put it, but finally, Tess blurted out, "So I guess Cade's like a cocaine dealer or something."

There was silence for a moment.

"Sorry, what?" Jordan asked.

"Well, I'm not really sure. All I know is he had drugs, and he got kicked out. Two other players claimed he tried to sell to them. It seems really stupid, but there were weird things about Cade, and I guess I didn't know everything about him..." Her voice trailed off, and she looked back at her bed. Her stomach felt unsettled.

"Well, what the hell does Cade have to say about it?" Tara asked angrily. She sounded ready to take him down, though she was the size of a toothpick.

"I haven't talked to him."

"What?" Andrea looked stunned. "Tess, you've talked to the guy for days on end. Literally, more than you've talked to me, and you're not gonna call and ask what actually happened?"

"I want to," Tess said, her voice trembling. "But thinking that he lied to me...it just makes me feel sick. And I can't respect drugs, either. With what happened to me...I just don't get it. Why would someone be healthy and choose to change that? It makes me see him differently."

"I should probably tell you I've done acid," Tara said casually.

"What?" Jordan, Andrea, and Tess all seemed to share the same shock.

"What? I'm an art major. It's like dessert for us."

Tess rolled her eyes and Andrea and Jordan just laughed.

"I'm just saying, Tess," Tara continued gently. "People do drugs. It doesn't automatically make them a horrible person. Plus, if they become addicted, it's no longer a choice."

After all the threats, Tess was surprised to hear Tara stand up for Cade. She didn't think less of Tara for experimenting. It didn't make her feel sick that she had chosen to do that to herself. It was her body, after all. But it wasn't like Tara brought it on a trip with her and tried to sell it, especially with millions of dollars on the line.

"I'm not ignorant to that, Tara," Tess said. "It's just...no offense, but I didn't expect it from Cade. It changes what I thought I knew about him."

"Well," Jordan said, "you didn't want to know too much before. I asked about his job and stuff, remember?"

"I know, I know..." Tess said. "I just thought it was simple the way things were. I didn't expect anything illegal."

Tara opened her mouth to speak.

Tess hurriedly continued, "And yes, Tara, I know people do illegal things sometimes, and I still care about them."

Tara closed her mouth.

Andrea shook her head. "It was completely stupid and irresponsible for him to have the drugs there, no matter what the explanation is. I'm glad you are safe after all of that, it could have easily turned dark. And I can't believe you had to compete alone."

"I agree with Andrea, if he really had the drugs there and was doing them, he could have ended up implicating you or he could have hurt you while he was high," Jordan said.

The four of them sat in silence with the heaviness of that for a moment.

"You still kicked ass competing alone though!" Tara said, attempting to lighten the mood.

"What was he like?" Jordan asked. "...before the whole getting caught with drugs thing."

Tess gazed out the window thoughtfully. Her voice was dreamy. "He was confident and kind. He talked to everybody. He really knew me well, and I guess we had chemistry."

"Did you..." Jordan began.

"Sleep with him?" Tara finished the sentence bluntly.

Tess blushed. She knew the question was coming. Her voice started soft, "Yeah. I thought this was something...like something people write stories about. I don't know, he was just...everything just felt right. And you were right, Tara, it felt natural." Tess shook her head, and her tone became bitter.

"But now, I just feel like an idiot. The idea of 'meant to be' makes me want to vomit out every cheap rom-com I've ever consumed."

"God, that's got to make it so much worse," Jordan said, and Andrea cringed at the words.

"Well, I think you need to call him." Andrea seemed to reach her verdict. "Even if you don't forgive him—which I'm not saying you should—I think you deserve an explanation."

Jordan chimed back in. "I'd say screw Cade, but you already did that...".

Tess couldn't help her miserable laugh.

"Still..." she continued. "I guess I'd want to know what actually happened if it was me. Maybe he was set up."

"You already showed him what's up with your solo performance. Now you're alpha when you call him," Tara said. She seemed to agree with the rest of her friends—Tess should call Cade.

They stayed on the phone for a while longer, Tess's spirits lifted as they talked about the game and the other players she'd met. Whenever Cade came up, Tess felt like she was telling an expired story, but the girls still enjoyed the bit about Times Square.

Jordan suggested Tess sell out Cade to the press for 'bonus prize money', but Tess didn't consider it for a moment. Whatever the story was with Cade, she understood wanting to keep private life private. She just felt relieved that she had kept her mental health her own story.

After hanging up, she sampled the array of room service that had arrived. It was hard to thoroughly enjoy the food with how her stomach felt, but she still had hunger pains to satisfy. Eventually, she went to her list of blocked numbers and removed Cade.

She hit the call button, and the phone rang twice. Those two rings felt like an eternity, during which Tess considered hanging up and throwing her phone out the window, flushing it down the toilet, or perhaps simply smashing it with something heavy. Her plans were cut short when Cade answered the phone.

"Well, the third-party queen has finally decided to grace me with a phone call."

She scolded herself for smirking at the title. So, Cade had watched the tournament. Of course, Cade had watched the tournament.

"You lied to me." It was all she could manage. She wasn't sure what someone was meant to say in this situation. She also didn't know what words would set off the burning in her eyes that would surely give way to tears.

"I didn't lie, Tess," Cade said quietly, "I made horrifically dumb decisions. I left you hanging at the worst time possible. I fucked up majorly. But I didn't lie to you. I didn't mean to lie to you."

She never heard this raw tone from Cade—his ego was nowhere to be found. Some firmness in her stance loosened, but she reminded herself he still had a lot to explain.

She took a deep breath and then asked, "Did you try to sell drugs to those two players? Danny and whoever."

"They mentioned an after-party they were planning, and they talked about wanting coke. And I said...I said I'd be good for it." He paused; the silence heavy.

She laid back on the bed in defeat. Some part of her was still hoping the drugs were magically planted. That it was all a setup.

Cade continued, "Look, I'm not proud of it, Tess, but I had it, and they didn't seem like the type to set me up like that."

Tess turned and laid on her stomach. "God, why would you even have the drugs?"

"It's common where I'm from. I used to sell. The video game income was getting me out, but I still used sometimes. I was still addicted. I still am addicted."

Tess closed her eyes. She continued softly, "Why didn't you tell me?"

"I don't know, Tess. You're just so perfect, and you have it all together."

Tess contained a bitter laugh.

"I didn't think you would understand. Everyone back home knows me for the drugs, and it was nice, for once, having someone who didn't know about them. Who saw me differently.

And I really liked you...I really like you. I didn't want to screw it up."

The desire to be known differently sounded all too familiar. She placed a hand on her pulsing head. "Were you high when we...?"

"No. God, no."

Tess breathed a sigh of relief. "I really liked you too..."

"Liked?" Cade's voice was smaller than ever before.

She sat back up in the bed. "I don't know, Cade. I'm really confused. I hated you this morning, but I missed you even when I won. And I'm not perfect. I haven't told you everything—"

"You don't have to," Cade quickly cut in. "I'm sorry. This is all my fault. I'm going to rehab. I've been avoiding it. I even used this tournament as an excuse to push it off, but I'm going to go now. Even if I didn't want to, the law is making sure of that. They let me out on bail, but I need to complete treatment and prove that I can recover to get the charges dropped."

Tess gripped the comforter and kept her voice firm. "I'm taking a spot with EFN. I don't want to duo with you anymore."

"I'm happy for you."

She didn't want him to be. In fact, she wanted him to argue with her and tell her that she needed to stay his duo. Then she wanted to say that she would and that she could forgive him. But it was all too raw. She really hated thunder.

"I'm going to miss you," she said.

"You have my number."

That didn't mean she was going to call.

"Tess," he said gently, "you can hate me, but you can also clearly place without me. You're brilliant, and your career's going to be brilliant."

Why did he have to say things that made it hard for her to remember why she didn't trust him?

"I'm glad you want to get better," she said, "...and I wish you the best."

She hung up before he could make it any harder. She contemplated blocking his number again—just to keep temptation away—but she figured she wouldn't be hearing from him either way. She had made herself pretty clear.

Tess walked to the bathroom and looked at her pills. She couldn't trust all these people who were trying to guide her in life, and she was sick of being treated like she was sick, like she couldn't make her own decisions. She didn't need anyone telling her what to do. She didn't need therapy.

Ever since she stopped focusing on the manic episode, it started to seem unreal—something that didn't really happen and wouldn't happen again. This was a turning point in her life. She would no longer rely on anyone or anything, only herself.

She picked up the pill bottle, unscrewed the cap, and shook the pills upside down over the toilet. The water splashed as they plopped in, one by one. When the bottle was emptied, she flushed and began to run the water for a bath.

What a way to celebrate her placement in the tournament, she thought as she submerged herself underneath the water.

Chapter Twenty-Two
What's Best

Tess excused herself as she passed a young man and slid into her window seat on the plane. He pulled in his legs and grimaced at her, then quickly shoved on his headphones. Tess tried not to display her relief—she would not have to make forced small talk with the guy. She had already spent the morning on forced conversations, from the call with EFN to back-to-back interviews with video game news channels.

Finally, her time in New York had ended, and she had never been so happy to be headed for her quiet suburbs in North Carolina. Four days had felt like a lifetime.

In the morning, Tess had signed a one-year contract with EFN. It would begin in three weeks. She would be a duo with someone else they had just picked up. He hadn't competed at the Grand Championship, so she had yet to meet him, but soon they'd be spending a lot of time together. She would have to stream as well, which she wasn't elated about, but it was a worthy trade-off for representation from a real organization.

Tess buckled her seatbelt as she noticed the flight attendants making rounds, then threw on her own headphones.

She'd half expected to wake up speaking nonsense today without the medication. But she didn't; she felt normal. If anything, she felt even better than before. The sting of Cade's decision was wearing farther away. Sometimes, certain things would happen that reminded her of their moments together—

moments that acted as kindling to that burning fire. But it was still burning weaker than the day before, and it would only die down more.

Great things had happened in New York, but terrible things too. It was swarming with video game fanatics, and she couldn't wait to return to a sense of anonymity. At this point, New York felt like a crowded maze, swallowing her from every direction. Closing in like the zone in DuskCabins. There was no way to get a break in that city. Nowhere to breathe.

The plane began to pick up speed, and she braced herself for departure.

"I'm proud of you," Tess's mother said as she helped her lift her carry-on into the minivan trunk. It was the middle of a Tuesday. Her father was at work, her brother was at school, but her mother had taken the day off just to meet her at the airport.

"Thanks, Mom." Tess slammed the trunk shut and moved toward the passenger seat. They pulled away from the pickup area, and Tess leaned her head against the window. The bare highways in Charlotte never looked so good.

"Did you even know what was going on when you watched the tournament?" Tess asked.

"I had no idea what I was watching," her mother admitted.

Tess laughed. "I figured."

"Your father seemed to understand it more. He used to play those kinds of games when they were first coming out, and your brother was really excited!"

Tess smiled at the thought of her angsty teenage brother rooting for her from home. He would never admit it to her. She knew that much.

"Was it hard to remember to take your medications?"

Tess exhaled and glanced out the window. Small hills bordering the highway seemed to move away as they sped by. She contemplated what she would tell her mother; what she *could* tell her mother.

"Not too hard," she said finally.

"Well one great thing about the tournament being over is: you have time to get back to therapy."

How quickly they were back to that version of Tess—the sick one. Not the victor. Did her mother not understand everything she had just accomplished alone?

"Actually," Tess said. "I signed a contract with an Esports organization, EFN. I'm going to be really busy. And I've been thinking...what happened earlier this year, maybe it was a one-time thing. I've never ended up like that before, even if I've been high or low—it's never been that extreme. Maybe they were wrong with the bipolar diagnosis. I mean, I haven't been going to therapy, and I feel fine...maybe better—"

"Tess, you're scaring me."

Tess frowned, frustrated first, to be interrupted and second, to be invalidated. Her mother was victimizing herself in an experience that didn't even belong to her. What happened to Tess was something she had gone through alone. How was someone else supposed to understand what she needed?

"I don't know how that scares you," Tess said sharply.

Her mother gripped the steering wheel so hard that her knuckles turned white. "Your father and I were the ones who brought you to the hospital. We had to see you in that state. I don't ever want to see you like that again. Do you know what it's like for a mother to—"

This time it was Tess that cut her mother off. "I get it was hard for you, but I don't feel like that anymore. I feel better."

Tess stared out the window. They pulled off on an exit toward their town. Memories started to flood back. The slipping of her thoughts into theories. The all-consuming paranoia, the way it ate away at her sense of reality.

But she had been stressed at college. It was just a breakdown. An atypical breakdown, sure. But not one that would define her life forever. It was over.

"I want you to stay better, Tess. Bipolar, it's something you have to treat—"

"For life. Yeah, I know; I read the pamphlets too. I just don't know that they were..." Right. She stopped herself. She didn't want to have this argument with her mother. It wouldn't go anywhere. She would just have to prove it with time. "Look, I'm just not ready to go back to therapy. That's all."

Her mother glanced at her warily. "You could talk to someone about what happened with Cade."

"Why the fuck would I want to do that?"

"Tess, language!" her mother snapped, but then she took a breath and proceeded carefully. "It had to be hard. Therapy can help you process things like this. For someone like you...it might be even harder to cope with this than the average person."

"Someone like me? Do you mean someone completely unstable and in need of intensive medications and therapy? Mom, do I look like I need those things? I handled this trip on my own. I handled what happened with Cade. I still competed. I'm not the same girl I was during my breakdown, and I don't want to be treated like I'm that girl forever."

Her mother shook her head. "That's not what I meant, Tess. A lot of people go to therapy. You don't have to be in an extreme state to need to process life."

Tess crossed her arms. "I'm done with this conversation. I'm an adult, and I'll go back to therapy when I want to. I think I've been handling things pretty well on my own."

They stopped at a red light and her mother sighed in defeat. "I just want what's best for your health."

"I do too," Tess huffed and stared out the window.

What was best for her health was to limit unnecessary medications. It wasn't digging through the past, blowing on fading embers that might catch fire. It was to move on and smother those bitches—forget any of this stuff ever happened.

It was to start her new career and focus on that instead. It was to get to a place where she could hear Cade's name and not feel her heart drop and to get there some other way than ruminating. It was to prove that she could depend on herself. Only herself.

Finally, the car lurched to a stop in front of their home, and Tess jumped out, grabbing her luggage without saying another word. Inside, she stared at the kitchen table where a cake was sitting on the counter. Sprawled across in blue icing, it said, "Congratulations." Carrot, her favorite type, and iced with her mother's unmistakable cursive script.

The front door opened again behind her, and her mother brushed past her and headed for the stairs. "Hope you don't mind cream cheese icing," she muttered, clearly just as upset from the conversation in the car, if not more.

Tess stood in silence, staring at the cake. She knew her mother was trying to look out for her, but Tess had to stand up for herself. It was up to her to decide what was right for her. Once she was off the medication for a while, she could clue her mother in. Then she'd see.

Tess didn't need anybody else taking care of her—no parent, no therapist, no drugs, and certainly no duo. She cut herself a piece of the cake and wondered how things would be with her new partner.

Chapter Twenty-Three
Fade to Interviews

Two weeks after returning from the tournament, Tess sat on a stool in a local art shop, watching Tara adjust a sunflower painting for the thirteenth time. Tara wore colorful patchwork overalls, and her long dark hair swooshed behind her as she stepped back and tilted her head. The room smelled of oil paint, and canvases covered every crevice, organized by theme—from nature to science fiction.

"Is it in line with the daffodils?" Tara asked, spinning to face Tess with wide eyes.

"Yes. And I think it was also in line on adjustments four, seven, and eleven," Tess replied flatly.

Tara stuck out her tongue and turned back toward the wall. She extended her arm and cupped her hand in front of the two paintings. "I just want it to be perfect for the show tomorrow." She glanced toward the store camera, then cupped her lips and added in a whisper, "Plus, Alice has been on my ass about how important the guests will be."

"At least you're not the only one with a boss on their ass," Tess replied, crossing her arms.

The best part of the contract with EFN was that Tess still got to play video games for a living. The worst part, however, was Tess could no longer dodge interviews. Before the Grand Championship, she had the choice to turn them down—a choice she exercised quite liberally. Now, not only did she have to accept every interview, but EFN was also signing her up for even more.

"You were meant to whisper that," Tara said, exasperated. She leaned over and picked up another painting—this one of a hummingbird and a cardinal sitting on either side of an oak tree, separated by the trunk. "What time is your next interview, anyway?"

"It's in two hours," Tess replied.

Tara spun on her heel, eyes nearly budging out of their sockets. "What the hell are you still doing here?"

Tess shrugged. "Spending quality time with one of my best friends."

Tara narrowed her eyes. "There is nothing quality about watching me stress over interior decoration." She gestured around the room and wiped a bead of sweat from her forehead.

Tess sighed, her shoulders slumping as she stared down at the wooden floor. "I get so nervous before interviews. Anything's better than sitting at the computer and waiting for the call." She looked back up at Tara, who wore a sympathetic expression.

"Why don't you help me with this one?" Tara said gently.

Tess crossed the room and scanned the wall for an open space wide enough. The place was seriously packed. She pointed to a gap between two abstract pieces. Tara shook her head and pointed to another spot between a park scene and a beachfront.

"The colors match better here," she said.

Tess rolled her eyes. "Why'd you even ask me?" she teased.

"I'm trying to help with your nerves, but not at the cost of my gallery," she said lightly. She frowned and looked back at Tess. "Maybe distraction isn't the best method. What kind of questions do you want to avoid? I'll ask you them now, and we can figure out how to answer them. Then, if they come up, you're already prepared."

Tess closed her eyes, then mimicking the accent of an old-times news reporter, said, "Is it true your partner Cade was disqualified from the tournament for possession of illegal substances?"

Although she avoided the questions while in New York, the media had caught up to the charges. According to the latest reports, Cade was still in an inpatient rehab facility in California. Tess didn't know if he had access to his phone, but she hadn't tried calling him. It was hard to forget how dangerous the situation could have been for her. And it was harder to forgive.

Tara sucked in a breath. "The hard hitters then. Has anyone asked you that so far?"

"Not word for word," Tess said.

A bell chimed at the front of the store, and Tara's gaze snapped forward. An elderly woman walked in, leaning her body against a metal walker. She squinted her eyes as her head swiveled around the shop.

"How can I help you?" Tara asked, approaching the entrance where the woman stood.

"I need a custom frame made for my granddaughter. Can you help with that?" Her voice was frail and soft.

"Sure, I can help you with that," Tara said. She gestured toward the front desk. "Follow me over here."

As they crossed the store, Tara mouthed to Tess, *this is going to take a while*. Her expression was apologetic, but Tess just waved her off. She couldn't expect Tara to neglect her job just because she was anxious.

Tess stepped outside the shop, the door jingling shut behind her. She thought about the many times that Cade had calmed her down when she was anxious. The meet-and-greets before the tournament had been so much easier with him beside her. The solo interviews felt heavier—something she had to carry all alone.

If only he could be with her for these interviews. If only he hadn't let her down.

Tess opened the camera application on her computer and immediately frowned. She patted down some flyaways and took a deep breath. A lavender candle on her dresser filled the room with a comforting scent that always helped to calm her. She lit the candle every time she took a virtual interview.

Within the camera frame, her room looked spotless. She had carefully adjusted the webcam to keep her bed—and the growing pile of clothes she was neglecting—out of view. Her interview application began to ring. Tess took one more deep breath, then clicked 'Accept'. She forced a smile as the video call connected. A middle-aged man appeared on the other end of the call, with a mousey appearance and a thick brown mustache.

"And now we are joined by EFN's newest recruit, Tess Calbaugh—or, as some of you may know her, JustATesst"

He paused as if waiting for applause, but the interview was being streamed on Twitch. There wouldn't be a live reaction.

Tess couldn't bear the silence any longer. She jumped in, "So happy to be here…" Shit. She didn't know the interviewer's name. Her eyes darted around the screen, but her brain couldn't process any of the words in her panicked state. "…and to be joining EFN."

The interviewer didn't seem fazed. He picked the conversation right back up. "And we're happy to have you here," he said. "For those of you who don't know, Tess participated in the Grand Championship as a contestant in duo DuskCabins, but at the last minute, her teammate was disqualified."

Tess winced. So, they were dropping right into it. She hated how matter of fact he spoke about what had happened with Cade. It had taken such an emotional toll on her, and he summarized it as if it were a quick piece of gossip.

The interviewer didn't register her reaction—or perhaps he just didn't care. "In the end, Tess competed as a solo player against forty-nine duos and still placed tenth. What a feat! Tess, can you walk us through how you prepared for the tournament? I think people really underestimate the work that goes into being a competitive Esports player."

Tess exhaled. The question was mild compared to the introduction. "To prepare for the tournament, Cade and I…"

The interviewer's eyes lit up as if her statement had just given him permission to breach the topic of Cade. She felt like slapping herself in the face, but luckily, she was sat on top of her hands and was able to suppress the instinct. She did not mean to mention Cade, but slipping into the memory of preparing for the tournament brought him right up.

She cleared her breath and continued, "I studied pro player strategies, kept up with the game updates so I could capitalize on the changes, and played for hours on end daily."

"You mentioned that you prepared with Cade. How did it feel when you were informed of his disqualification and told you would have to play solo?"

He asked the question as if he was asking about her favorite color—not the moment she learned her partner betrayed her.

Tess felt her throat tighten as she thought back to the morning of the tournament and instantly felt her eyes water. She forced her mind blank to prevent the onslaught of tears. There was no reason she had to tell the truth.

"I was shocked," she said evenly, "but determined to do the best I could—with or without a partner."

The interviewer frowned as if the answer didn't have enough juice for him. He let the silence hang, allowing Tess the opportunity to elaborate. She didn't.

"And you still did great!" he said eventually.

The interview pressed on with simpler questions. What did Tess think of New York? What excited her most about joining EFN? What was her advice for aspiring Esports competitors? She provided much more elaborate answers to questions she felt were more appropriate, and that seemed to guide the interviewer in the right direction. A lifetime later, the call ended, and she signed off.

As soon as the monitor faded to black, her mind wandered right back to the question the interviewer had asked about the morning of the tournament. This time she didn't forcer herself to avoid feeling it. Warm tears cascaded down her cheeks as her thoughts moved to the conversation with Cade. She wanted so badly to believe it was a setup or a misunderstanding. But he made it clear that wasn't the case. It was his fault.

Her efforts to keep the situation out of her mind were fruitless, as all these interviews brought it right back to the surface. She wiped her cheek and stared at the flame flickering in her candle.

In a week she'd get to start playing with someone new. All she could do was hope that her next duo would fill the void Cade had left behind and the media would move on with time. Cade would become a distant memory, just like the mania.

Chapter Twenty-Four
Preferring Chemistry to Physics

Tess had a decent assault rifle, some armor, a sniper rifle, and three grenades. She was at a small distance from Nathan—or, rather, EFN Firebringer. Over the last two weeks, he made it very clear that he preferred to be called Firebringer, and yet she felt ridiculous when she addressed him aloud. At this point, she simply avoided calling him by name, even if it put a damper on their communication.

"Up ahead, Justice," he called back to her. She held in a sigh and ran after him. He also insisted on calling her by her username, but he pronounced it all wrong. She realized that correcting him was a moot point after the fourth attempt.

The opposing duo came into render distance, cutting through the woods en route to the factories. Tess fired off a few rifle shots. She did some damage, but they began to build a defense.

"Cover me, I'm pushing in," Nathan said. A command, not a suggestion.

He charged ahead, pulling out a shotgun. Tess didn't have one yet. If it had been Cade, he would have swapped the shotgun for her sniper rifle. On the other hand, Nathan liked to get into the action as much as she did. Now, she found herself covering from a distance much more than she used to.

She brought a wall around her for cover and built a ramp to peer over the top. She continued to lie in with the assault rifle shots as Nathan pushed his way in. He built rapidly against the duo, and they tried to contest, but his reaction time was significantly superior. Hers would be too, she thought, if he ever allowed her to be at the front of the action. From where she stood, it was hard to do anything other than continue shooting down the wooden structures. She couldn't even see an opponent.

"Keep pressure," he yelled.

She rolled her eyes and kept shooting. What else was she gonna do? Turn around and head to the bars in Metropolis?

Finally, Nathan fired his shotgun twice. Both players were immediately pronounced dead on her screen. Tess descended from her own structure and ran over to the remnants of the fight to see what she could scavenge from the kills.

"Oh, god. I'm too fucking good." His voice was full of ecstasy—somehow the same dose for every kill. Tess tried to bring him down to earth the first few times but quickly learned he did not take well to being teased. She just chose not to comment anymore.

To Tess's delight, a common shotgun with a stash of ammo was left behind. She dropped her sniper rifle, taking the shotgun in its place.

"Alright, zone's closing in over the woods. There are two players left. We're scrapping the factories and heading in for the last fight. You keep the distance. I'll go in." He started moving without waiting for so much as a head nod.

"I've got a shotgun now. We could both push in," Tess suggested, following quickly behind. She turned to check behind them occasionally for signs of the remaining opponents.

"We could, but it will be easier for me to 1v2 with ranged pressure."

Why did he say 1v2 as if Tess wasn't even in the game? She sighed and swapped her shotgun back for her assault rifle. She visualized the income EFN would send to her bank account and the stream revenue. It was easier to be patient with Nathan with that in mind. They finished the game similarly to their earlier fight, and the victory screen flashed.

VICTORY: EFN FIREBRINGER AND EFN JUSTATESST

Tess hurriedly backed out and blinked past the scoreboard. Nathan had eighteen kills. She had one. A single lucky sniper shot during a brief moment of bliss where he wasn't begging her for backup.

If the score considered how many structures a player had knocked down, it would be a different story. Tess felt like her child was dying every time she played with Nathan. Her child being her kill-death-assist ratio.

The worst part was that he wasn't bad. The first couple of days they'd played together, they had versed each other and found themselves pretty equivalent in straight building and shooting skills. Shortly after, Nathan began to refuse this kind of practice. He said he preferred to practice on the same team, the way that they would compete, but she suspected it had more to do with the live stream.

His chat certainly had a lot to say about the rounds that went to Tess. She also had her own chat, which she completely ignored despite feedback from EFN saying audience engagement could boost her ratings and donations.

It was five now, and her contracted stream time was up for the day. She switched tabs on her computer, moving to the streaming software that EFN provided. She grinned as she clicked: End Stream. It was her favorite button.

Nathan's contracted time was also up, but she noticed his Twitch stream was still running.

"Another easy victory. God, I was made to play this game. Oh, Justice, great cover. Good thing I got you following me around!"

"Yep, see you tomorrow." She tried to keep her voice neutral but doubted he would notice either way. Without waiting for a response, she exited the voice chat and shut down her computer. She sighed in relief at the sound of silence—at this point, she was sick of the DuskCabins music.

Across the room, on her dresser, a notepad sat open. She had been writing a lot recently, with new ideas about almost everything flowing constantly. The notebook was filling up fast. Tess crossed the room and then jotted down some things that crossed her mind as they played today.

- Type of instrument that doubles as a weapon in DUSKCABINS
    o Mind control device
- Game w/ battle royal but animals
    o Different animal kingdoms
    o Evolution
        ▪ Do research on evolution
- A story about escaping a video game that keeps restarting
    o Being stuck with an obnoxious duo
        ▪ (Nathan)

She glanced around her room as she wrote the final words, then looked back at the notebook. Something made her skin crawl. It felt like once she had put those thoughts down on paper, they would float through the wind and make their way to Nathan. Or worse, to the EFN staff that placed her with him just two weeks ago.

▪——(Nathan)

"Just in case of magical word transmitters..." she said dismissively.

She laughed at the ridiculous thought, but there was an intoxicating bliss that came with such a strange, outlandish idea. She jumped as her phone rang and then smiled at herself once more. She closed the notebook and then picked up the video call from Andrea.

"Well, well, well—how's our famous streamer?" Andrea asked. On the other end, she stood in her kitchen, putting together dinner, still dressed in work clothes.

"Just thinking about this story: a girl gets trapped in a video game with an obnoxious duo and can't escape." Tess crossed the room as she spoke and flopped down onto the bed.

Andrea chuckled. "Ahh, reminds me of a friend."

"Shh, don't make it too obvious. We don't know who's listening in on this call."

Tess was half-joking, but she also wondered if EFN could monitor her calls. Or, if not, there was always the FBI agent theory. It was a meme, but the idea had to come from somewhere.

"I take it things aren't getting better with Nathan?"

Tess dropped her head in her palms. "I don't even enjoy the game anymore. It's like torture."

"I stopped by your stream, 40,000 people. You've got to be raking in the money." Andrea pulled out a measuring cup and began to pour flour inside.

"I keep reminding myself of that." Tess sighed. At what point would her happiness mean more than the money? Her contract had her playing with Nathan all day, and afterward, she didn't want to play anymore. She wanted to log off and focus on other things. "It's just like if I'm a cog in this machine that spouts out green paper that people assign meaning to, but I don't have a meaning...is that living? Or—"

Andrea dropped the flour box onto the counter and looked into the phone. "Girl, what the fuck are you taking? And can I have some of it?"

Tess laughed. She honestly had no idea what she was talking about, but it seemed like an idea she could work with later. She

jolted up from her bed, reopened the notebook, and jotted it
down.

- Money machine with different meanings than its
  parts meanings.

She returned to her phone, where Andrea had resumed
cooking, and realized she was hungry herself. She wondered what
she could make tonight. With the return to work, her mother had
been cooking less frequently. Still, every morning, without fail,
Tess found her water glass refilled on her bedside table. She
glanced at it now, full on her bedside table.

Tess continued to drink the water, so her mother had not
caught on to the fact that she had given up the medication. Tess
had yet to feel anything other than better. She was even less tired.
Soon enough, she could clue the others in.

"So, does it make you miss him?"

Tess's gaze snapped back to her phone. Andrea was now
stirring her ingredients inside a metal bowl, and she looked at
Tess expectantly. Andrea knew to avoid this topic, yet she was
choosing to push Tess. Why she was pushing her was unclear.

"I try not to think about him," Tess said quietly.

"It's been what—six weeks? I know how much you cared for
him. You must want to talk about it. You went through so much
with him."

"I don't like digging into the past. It's unproductive." Tess
laid back on the bed, her head resting against a purple fluffy
pillow.

"How can you go through all these hardships without even
talking about them?" At this point, she seemed to be referring to
more than just Cade. Tess wondered if her mother had mentioned
the conversation about therapy to Andrea.

Tess threw her hands in the air. "Because talking about
things is…"

"Difficult?" Andrea suggested.

Tess crossed her arms. "Pointless."

"Necessary to healing?"

"Prolonging to hurt."

Andrea frowned. "Has he tried to reach out to you?"

"No." Tess attempted to sound indifferent and gazed sideways out her bedroom door.

"If you don't want to think about him, why are you disappointed that he hasn't contacted you?"

Tess narrowed her eyes at the phone. Andrea had ditched the stirring and stood closer to the camera, hands on her hips. There was a light sound of construction in the background at her apartment.

"I'm not. It's exactly what I asked of him."

"Tess, I know you too well. Come on."

Tess sighed and sat up. "I don't want to let my intolerance of this new duo blind me to what Cade actually did. I don't know that I miss him. Maybe I'm just displacing my feelings."

Andrea pointed her wooden spoon at the camera. "Well, as your best friend, I can tell you that you miss him." She paused for a moment, then moved back to stirring her bowl. Tess tried to consider her feelings. Maybe Andrea had a point. Andrea continued, "I think you would miss him with or without Mr. Firebringer, and I think you should process what happened…"

"If you say in therapy—"

"In general," Andrea interrupted. "Call him. Take precautions of course and use your judgement to make sure he's truly giving up the drugs. You don't need to go sleep with him again, but you don't have to let this thing ruin your friendship."

"I don't know…"

"Tess, addiction isn't a thing people generally want to be struggling with. And as you know, getting help isn't easy, but you said he was doing it. Maybe you should give him the chance to change. With all your bipolar…requirements…maybe you could under—"

"But that's the thing. He had a choice, and I didn't. Besides, I'm better now. I don't even think I need the medications, actually."Andrea glanced back at the camera, a confused expression flickering across her face. "Don't need them? But didn't your doctors say that you had to take them for the rest of your life?"

Tess played with her necklace. "Yeah, but lately...I've been feeling like maybe they were wrong."

Andrea frowned, but she didn't seem to know what to say. Tess didn't want to wait around for her to come up with a response. She was sure it wouldn't be anything close to agreement.

"Look, I'm really hungry. I'll talk to you about it more later."

"Alright," Andrea's voice was uncertain.

Tess hung up before she could say anything else, then downed the water on her bedside table. She returned the empty cup and headed downstairs to make some food. Her thoughts shifted away from the conversation fast. She wondered instead: Was it possible that vegetables experienced emotion, but we just don't know about it?

Chapter Twenty-Five
A Water Slide

Tess blinked at her ceiling and rolled over again in her bed. The ceiling was decorated with glow-in-the-dark stars. They had been stuck up there when she was six or seven, perhaps, and never came down. Even now, she liked the idea of a galaxy hanging just above her, suspended between the room and the plaster ceiling. She didn't care if that was childish.

Outside her window, crickets chirped in a sort of symphony. She imagined they were dressed in miniature tuxedos for the performance. A giggle escaped from her lips. After a moment, the smile was replaced by a deep exhale. It was long past her call with Andrea, yet she still couldn't shake the thought of Cade.

Night by night, sleep was getting harder and harder to attain. Perhaps her body was just adjusting to being off the medication. Her PC hummed in the corner of her bedroom, and the rainbow keyboard lit up like a night light.

It was like having a little pet, she thought. A goldfish computer. He kept her company, and she would remember to feed him—unlike the real goldfish she'd had at thirteen. She still felt guilty about that to this day. At least this goldfish just had to be plugged in.

She jumped up suddenly from her bed and powered on the monitor. She pulled up a YouTube video of goldfish swimming inside a tank and set it to full screen. She left it playing on a loop and sat back in bed, but her mind buzzed too rapidly for her to lay still. Thinking about guilt made her think about Cade. Why? He was the one who crossed her.

It was nice having someone that didn't know. Who saw me differently.

She had gone stone cold at that statement when, in reality, she should have softened. She had felt precisely the same way. She could have told him right there and then, but she didn't. He was like a goldfish she could have fed.

She looked over at the screen. "Cade?" The goldfish stared back at her with dull eyes. He wasn't very responsive.

No, it was highly unlikely that Cade would be the goldfish in the computer. She was jumping from A to B to C. She had been doing that a lot recently, hence the journal. Her eyes moved to the dresser, where it sat. It wasn't like she was going to get sleep anytime soon. With a sigh, she swung her legs over the side of her bed and crossed the room.

- Why can't I stop thinking about Cade?
    - Guilty
        - ~~What if he was a goldfish~~
    - Sick
        - Addiction is being sick
    - ~~What if I made him sick?~~
    - What if I left him alone and sick?
    - What if Cade is dying?

Tess startled at her words. Cade was sick, and Tess was sure of it. She could feel it. They had a strong connection; she knew this. She just had chosen to ignore it after what he had done to her. But now she allowed herself to lean into the connection. And she could feel it. Something was wrong.

Cade had gone to get better but wouldn't because Tess was holding onto this bitterness. A bitterness that had evolved into something real. Something that made him physically ill. She knew how to make it better. It was obvious. She had to prove that she still cared. The problem was she hadn't reached out to him since leaving New York, and now he was far away in California.

Tears welled in her eyes. It was possible that Cade didn't even know he was dying. What were the chances of him believing her tale over the phone?

Tess moved back to her computer and closed the video of the goldfish. She looked at the time—it was two AM. She recalled a story Cade had told her about La Jolla Beach. He mentioned walking there after one of their wager games. She did some backtracking to find the nearest airport and then looked at the available flights.

Her adrenaline was rushing, and she felt like a real spy. She was the only one who knew Cade was sick, most likely, and she was the only one who could save him. It was her own secret mission. If she told her parents, they could interfere. If she told her friends, she'd have to explain herself, and there was simply no time. There was no way to explain it either. She just knew it. Deep in her bones, she felt it.

Without checking the price, she booked the next flight and sighed as a long form appeared on the screen. There was so much information zig-zagging its way through the world all the time, just to be purged later. Were there garbage men for that in the computers? What endless amounts of work they had piling up. She recoiled for a moment. Why did it have to be garbage *men*? How sexist of her.

A timer popped up on the screen to remind her to finish checking out. She spoke out loud as she carefully answered each question, trying to keep her attention still. Finally, she clicked confirm. The next screen displayed her departure time. She nearly fell out of the seat. She only had two hours.

Tess rushed to her closet and dragged out her carry-on but then felt a sense of panic at the thought of packing it up. Wouldn't bringing a small backpack and seeing where things go from there be more fun? She could collect items along the way, just like in DuskCabins. Spies did travel light, after all.

Tess collected a baseball cap, her notebook, and a light pink sweatshirt. She chose carefully, knowing these would be the tools that accompanied her on the journey of a lifetime. What else did spies need? Well, this spy would need to be transported to the airport fast. She grabbed her phone and pulled up a rideshare app. With the car on its way, Tess found a pen and quietly crept out of the house.

She sat cross-legged on the road at the bottom of the driveway, waiting for the driver. Something in her heart had lightened as soon as she realized Cade was sick. It felt good to forgive a little. She started to scribble more notes in her journal.

- Video game of goldfish
    - Fighting in battle royal
    - Being fueled by fish food
    - Robot goldfish fueled by electricity

A light flickered in the distance, and Tess slammed her journal shut. She didn't want anyone photographing her ideas. They could make the game before she did. She needed this game to succeed and get out of her current career.

The light moved closer. She nearly fell over laughing when she realized it was her ride. Not the paparazzi, then. Her video game secrets were safe for now. She hopped into the backseat, and they set off.

For such late travel, Tess had bounds of energy. She wondered if some people were born to be awake by night and others by day, but we all just fall into this daytime loop. She also considered that spies must run on adrenaline, and as one herself, she felt it.

At the airport, she happily spoke with staff and other passengers. The guy sitting next to her on the plane was flying in to interview for a tech internship. She had so many questions about his coding experiences, and he seemed happy to discuss them with her. He became more solemn when she mentioned that she was visiting a sick friend. She kept the details to herself, as a spy should.

They landed at 7:30 AM. She shot a quick text over to Nathan.

Tess: Feeling sick. Won't be on for games or stream.

The next order of business was her parents.

Tess: I forgot to mention, I am traveling for an EFN event. I left super early this morning. I'm sorry I forgot to warn you.

She tucked her phone away and continued through the airport. A small shop to her right was selling beach blankets, and she felt magnetized by the purple and pink braided material. She ran over.

Movement was coming from all directions, so Tess kept her eye out while she handed her card to the shopkeeper. You never knew who was sent to sabotage your spy mission. With the beach blanket stuffed into her backpack, Tess pulled out the rideshare app again. This time, the destination was La Jolla Beach.

When she finally laid down her blanket close to the entrance, the sun's glow was reflected in the sand. It was early enough that the beach hadn't really filled up. She texted Cade her location. Not too long after, he called, but she didn't pick it up. She needed to see him in person for this to work. That's why she had traveled here.

Cade: Tess, are you really in California right now?
Tess: Just meet me at the beach. I'll explain.
Cade: 15 Minutes

Fifteen minutes was no time for Tess. She laughed about time. It was a made-up concept. Surely someone somewhere could already time travel. She wondered if that was a thing that she could figure out. With all the A's to B's to C's, it seemed like something she could do. She watched the ocean's crashing waves and thought about it. With every crash she considered a new theory, and as the water receded branched it into another.

She scoffed at the ocean. So much time was wasted, pulling back and reflecting when the waves were done crashing. There was no time for Tess to pull back and reflect like the ocean. Not when there were new branches to be made. Imagine all that she could accomplish without ever stopping to reflect.

"Tess," Cade's voice carried through the warm breeze. "I am very happy to see you again...but why are you here?" His tanned skin was glowing in the sun, and his head stood just in front of the light, which formed a sort of halo around him.

Tess motioned for him to sit on the blanket with her. She prepared her next words carefully, and he watched her closely as she did, concern etched into his expression.

"I know you are sick, Cade..."

He laughed for a moment, and his shoulders loosened. He paused for a moment, observing that Tess still had a stone-cold expression.

He reassured her, "I'm not...as far as I'm aware. Got my flu shot and everything."

Tess laughed. "Not the flu, silly." Her voice faltered. "I'm here to...help you. It's my fault." She dropped her head into her hands. "I know it is."

His voice grew more serious. "Nothing that happened was your fault, Tess." He had that same heavy tone from after the tournament, the last time they spoke, the time she closed herself off from him and let him get sick.

"Cade, I lied to you. I said I never wanted to duo with you again. I was wrong. I was so wrong. And now you're dying,"

She lifted her face out of her palms to look back at him. His eyes were filled with concern, but they were soft. He wasn't angry with her for causing all of this. Was it possible she had already cured him with her presence? It was hard to tell if it worked. Tears started streaming down her face, and she looked at the ocean again. Searching for more A's, B's, and C's. It was too much to hold a life in your hands.

"And I'm scared. I'm really scared," she whispered.

Cade slipped an arm around her, and she leaned into his body. He smelled just like the salty atmosphere. She could hear his heartbeat, and it was steady. That was a good sign, she thought.

"Shh, Tess, it's alright. I'm not dying," he said gently. "Did you take something?"

She jerked out of his hold. "You don't believe me."

"No," he said quickly. "I believe you. I mean...I believe you believe you. I just—you're not making any sense, and I've been around people on drugs, I know—"

"I don't take any drugs. That's why I'm clear-headed. That's why I'm not flat and can save you."

It was true. If she were taking her medication, she may have never realized Cade was sick. And where would he be without her help? She shook her head, wishing she could understand the rules of this sickness. It was hard to tell if he was really cured.

"Okay," he said slowly. "So, no drugs. What do you mean you're not flat?"

"Ugh, Cade, there's no time for this."

How could he not feel the danger he was in? No wonder he didn't hold any grudge against her. No wonder this was a spy mission. It seemed he was not even aware of the dire circumstances. Only she understood the stakes.

"You've come all this way. Surely there is time."

Tess rolled her eyes. It was hard for others to keep up with her when she knew so much. Still, she elaborated. "It's just all these people are trying to smother me into this flat line. Therapists, doctors, family, and even my friends are in on it. And they do it with the drugs. Not like your kind of drugs. Legal drugs. But I've stopped taking them, just in time to realize how much danger you're in."

Cade exhaled carefully. "Right...and what's that danger again?"

Tess didn't answer out loud. An idea occurred to her. She leaned in and kissed Cade softly on the lips. He didn't move away, and as she leaned back, he raised an eyebrow at her. He looked somewhat amused, but she saw something else in his gaze. It was the same look that people had given her at school. The first time she had been manic.

But things were different this time. This was a life and death matter. She was lucky to have awakened to the reality in time to save him.

"I was making you sick with my lies," she said. "That's why I had to come here. I had to prove to you that I still care. I didn't want you to end up like my goldfish..."

She glanced around the beach nervously. It was starting to get more crowded, and she wasn't sure everyone there had good intentions. She whispered the rest, just in case. "I don't know if it worked. Do you believe me?"

"Yes, Tess, I believe you care," Cade said. He brushed a loose strand of blonde hair behind her ear, then hesitated. "Those legal drugs...when did you last take them?"

Tess scrambled to her feet and looked over her shoulder. Did he have a hidden microphone on? Were doctors waiting just beyond the dunes, ready to come pouring onto the beach? Would her parents show up and have her locked up again? Was this an MTV show she had never heard of, focused on finding people like her and making them flat? They must have been videotaping her for a while. She would need a lawyer and—

"Tess?" Cade stood up and put a hand on her arm. It brought her back to the current moment. "Sorry, you don't have to tell me."

She turned back slowly, studying his face. He looked healthy, and she smiled; the kiss must have worked. After a moment, she untensed, and they sat back down together.

The ocean crashed in the distance, the waves rhythmic and infinite. It was such a beautiful thing. She was struck by the urge to do more research about the ocean. What lived there? That could be fascinating. It was quite intriguing how beaches existed on their own anyway and how houses could be right there on them.

Tess always imagined herself in a city, but a beach like this could be a new dream. Or perhaps a city on a beach—only if pollution could be avoided. Or would that defeat the whole purpose of the beach?

A couple walked along the shoreline. After watching them for a moment, she glanced back to Cade. He studied her skeptically, seemingly lost in thought.

"Tess," he asked. "Don't you have practice today for EFN?"

She smiled deviously. "I told Nathan I was sick. Really, you were sick, so it was only a small lie." She tilted her head with a frown. "I don't think I want to play with him anymore. I haven't wanted to since the first game, but I'm still under contract. I'm going to find a way out. Sometimes stars say other things than lawyers, and the universe gets angrier when one isn't listened to— and it's not lawyers."

He stared back at her with the same concerned look. He was never too poetic, but she didn't know how to dumb it down anymore. The world wanted them to play together, and she knew that because it wanted her to know. Her avoidance thus far was only making him sick, and if she scared him away now, it wouldn't work either.

She jumped to her feet. "I've got to go."

"What? Where do you possibly need to go?"

"Somewhere my energy doesn't have the wrong effect at the wrong time," Tess said, backing away from the blanket. "I've cured you, but I don't want to scare you...I just don't know how to measure ingredients, and if it's a cake and the timings are wrong or the proportions are wrong, it just won't work out." She started laughing so hard she almost fell over. "I've never baked a cake in my life."

Tess recovered from her laughing fit and looked at Cade. He scanned the beach and stood up, shaking the sand out of the blanket.

"Where are you staying?" he asked.

Tess shrugged. "I'm not sure yet, but I figured that would be a fun problem to solve once I got here."

"Come back with me," Cade suggested softly. "I'll show you my place. I have a couch."

"If you insist," she said.

The wind gusted at their backs as they walked off the beach. Tess turned her face into the breeze and let her hair fly back in the breeze. What could Earth possibly be trying to tell her now?

Chapter Twenty-Six
A Fugitive

Cade's apartment was just a short walk from the beach. Every so often, Tess would stop to ask him questions about the buildings they passed. Cade answered distractedly. He seemed to be trying to hurry her along, though she couldn't figure out why. They were unlikely to be recognized; it wasn't like New York anymore.

Finally, they arrived at his building, took the elevator to the fifth floor, and stepped into a hallway.

"Isn't it weird that we take elevators completely for granted?" Tess mused as the door shut behind them.

"Entirely," Cade replied. He seemed less puzzled and more distracted, but Tess barely noted it as she continued.

"Imagine we were to appear in a world with no elevators. Who would even know how to make one again?"

"I imagine the same people who made them here," he said, smiling slightly.

Tess could tell he found this fun. Or perhaps he was happy to not feel sick anymore.

"Imagine if we all disappeared without them."

"I guess we'd all be getting a little more fit."

He stopped in front of a door, unlocked it, and pushed it open, motioning for Tess to walk through first.

The apartment was a little messy, which he apologized for, as he walked to the kitchen and began to move dishes to the sink. The entrance led into a small living area with a tattered couch and a large TV. A compact kitchen was connected to that room in the back, and a closed door that must have led to a bedroom.

Tess tossed her backpack on a table and then collapsed on the couch. It had been over thirty-six hours since she last slept, and her body felt tired, yet her mind was still spinning. It was like the two diverged in a yellow wood. "My mind took the path less traveled," she mumbled sleepily.

"What?" Cade called from the kitchen.

She started laughing again. He really wasn't one for poetry. Perhaps if she thought of rap lyrics that could explain the thought, but she hadn't listened to much. She only knew what he had played for her online, late at night after gaming. She tried to recall one of the songs, but her mind sped right past the train of thoughts and onto a new track. Back to drugs. Were there any here? Was her mission truly over?

She stood up and made her way casually through the room. She ran her hand along small items clustered around the TV, a bit of dust collected on top. She paused at an Xbox.

"You want to play Call of Duty?" Cade asked, peering through a window above the kitchen sink. "Sorry, it's not a Wii…"

Tess glanced over her shoulder, looking past Cade to his fridge. A calendar hung there, with two weeks crossed off. The first was one long line. The next week was covered in X's—one for each day this week, ending with yesterday.

He followed her gaze. "It's my inpatient rehab and outpatient participation days after. The days I've been clean," he said proudly but sheepishly. He reached for a pen and marked off the present day.

She smiled at him. It was so endearing he put his progress on the fridge, it reminded her of the elementary paintings that her mother would hang on their own fridge.

"Was it hard?" she asked slowly. "To listen to what other people thought was best for you?"

He considered her question for a moment. "Yes. I had to want to get better for myself. No one else could convince me. What happened at the Grand Championship was a rude awakening to the fact that I needed to change. There are things that will help me stay sober, though, like NA; it's a group where we can talk it through with others that understand."

Tess frowned. "Groups aren't for everyone."

She turned on the Xbox, grabbed a controller, and slouched on the couch. Cade made his way into the room and grabbed the other controller. He sat down beside her, looking thoughtful about her response.

"No," he agreed after a moment. "I guess it would be different if I didn't click with the people in the group. Or if I wasn't ready to work on myself."

"I was ready to work on myself. I just didn't want to dig into the past anymore." Tess crossed her arms. She didn't know how Cade knew so much.

"I didn't either. Not for a long time." Cade didn't look over. His eyes were fixed on the screen as he set up a custom match. "Really, not until I hurt you at the tournament."

"Cade, I feel like I really hurt you. I mean, that's why I came here after all. The illness."

Cade exhaled. "I keep trying to tell you, Tess. I only blamed myself." He tore his gaze from the game and looked at her. "If you want me to feel better, can you just tell me what you are on? So, I can help you."

She dropped her controller on the couch, and he flinched. She recoiled at the thought that she was hurting him again. Why couldn't she stop? Her eyelids felt heavy. This whole thing was exhausting. Did spies sleep?

"I told you, Cade. None. Do you not believe me?"

"It's not that I don't believe you," he said slowly. "...It's just that I know you better than this."

Tess leaned back against the couch and closed her eyes. "Is it alright if we just put the game on hold? I think I need a nap."

"Yeah, go ahead." He stood back up. "I'm going to run and grab some groceries, and I need to go to my outpatient group at eleven. Have you eaten today?"

She blinked. She hadn't even thought about eating, but now that he mentioned it, she was starving. She shook her head.

"I'll be back soon."

He left for the store, closing the door gently behind him, and Tess laid down on the couch. She pulled a blanket off the top and covered her body. The sleep crept in slowly, but it eventually came.

When she woke, the scent of pizza filled the apartment. Cade was watching her carefully from the kitchen. Something in his demeanor changed, but she couldn't figure out what. Tess took note of the cardboard oven pizza box.

"I love those pizzas. My mom makes them at home a lot," Tess said. She stretched her arms above her head and yawned.

He smiled. "That's great." His tone felt distant as if there was something he wasn't saying. Tess narrowed her eyes, but her phone buzzed inside her backpack, pulling away her attention. She crossed the room to check it.

Missed Calls from Andrea: 6

Andrea: Tess where's your stream today?

Andrea: Tess…why did your parents call and say you're on business in Cali?

Andrea: Tess, no offense, but I'm worried about how you were acting yesterday.

Andrea: Tess, I'm sorry.

Sorry for what? Tess glanced back at Cade, who wore a guarded expression. It seemed there was still something on his mind. The oven beeped, and he moved to pull out the pizza, then sliced through it slowly. Afterward, he set two slices on two plates.

Finally, he spoke. "Tess, I talked to Andrea."

"What?" Tess dropped her phone back on top of the bag.

"She found me on Venmo and sent a dollar with her phone number. The message said: 'Need to talk about Tess.'"

Tess blinked. "Why would she do that?"

"She's worried about you. She clued me in on some things. I get it now. You're not on drugs. I think you're…manic."

Tess frowned and walked to the kitchen. "So what? Do you want to send me to the hospital to get flattened?" She took her slice of pizza and chewed carefully. Her appetite was somehow lost and screaming all at once.

Cade didn't touch his own slices. "No, Tess, I just want to get you help. I know you feel scared, and I know what it's like to not feel in control."

What didn't he understand? She could never have saved him if she hadn't been in this state. How was she supposed to return to the numb feeling of before? There was so much more she was aware of now. Besides, the last time she went to the hospital, things got scary.

"They can't help me," she spoke in a quick panic. "Please, you can't take me."

"Tess, I didn't want to get the help I needed either. I didn't want to believe I had a problem until it went too far." He glanced around the apartment, then back at Tess.

She blinked as she realized what he was insinuating. "You don't want me here? This is too far…"

"No, I *do* want you here," Cade took a deep breath. "It's just the way you came here is a little extreme, and the reasoning doesn't make sense to me. Listen, you'll come with me if you want me to feel better. We'll go somewhere they can help you stabilize."

Tess began to shake her head. She wanted to argue that she didn't need to be stabilized. But Cade was right about one thing. She had come here to make sure that he would feel better, that he would be cured of whatever sickness she had caused. Now, he was telling her that for him to feel better, she needed to go to the hospital. How could she say no?

"I do want you to feel better. That's why I'm here," she resigned.

Cade placed a hand on her shoulder. "I will stay with you as long as they let me. And I'll visit until you're sick of me."

Tess touched his hand with her own. "I would never get sick of you."

Tears started spilling from her eyes. "Last time, it felt like they wanted to kill me," she whispered. "I try not to remember it. I try not to talk about it."

"I will check in on you. I will make sure that doesn't happen," he promised. "I have nothing better to do between NA and playing video games."

Tess hung her head in defeat. She wiped her tears away with her sleeve. "Can I finish my pizza?"

Cade laughed carefully and nodded.

Chapter Twenty-Seven
A Treaty

"Tess, we're having group."

A red-haired tech peaked her way into Tess's small room and continued down the hallway. Tess set her book down on the side table and swung her legs over the gym mattress they called a bed, walking toward the hallway. Her roommate was likely already there—a sweet woman in her fifties, a mother.

In the hallway, she smiled at the nurses who passed her. They smiled back. That hadn't always been the case. At first, when she arrived, the mania got worse. The delusions became darker, but the staff patiently worked her through it. After a few days, she came back to herself again. Afterward, she felt like she had to prove to them that she was a whole different person. Not normal, they had corrected her when she tried to dismiss her manic self, but *healthy*.

In the group room, she dropped into a chair next to a girl named Summer. Summer had short black hair and beautiful green eyes. Though she was the same age as Tess, she made it look easy to open up in the group and encouraged Tess to do the same. She didn't have bipolar disorder, but she'd been in and out of enough inpatient stays to understand it. Her validation made Tess feel less alone.

The copper-haired tech entered the room and took a seat. She gazed around the room and smiled. "Thanks, everyone, for showing up. I know the group is optional, but you are making the choice to participate, and that will make all the difference for you."

There were nods around the room.

"Today, I want to discuss plans for what comes after inpatient. As you all know, your mental health is something you will care for your entire life. It's important to be prepared. What are other things that help you outside the hospital?"

"Therapy," Summer answered first.

The tech nodded. "Exactly, that's a great one." She looked to the other side of the room. "What are some barriers to therapy? What stops us from going even though we know it helps?"

"Not having transportation," an older man suggested. He sat with his chair backed against one of the activity tables.

Tess frowned at herself, guilt coursing through her. She had a perfectly functioning car and still didn't go.

"Okay, right—exactly," the tech continued. "In that case, looking for a closer therapist is good. Someone you could reach from public transport or maybe ask a friend or family member to help get you there."

"Not being ready to talk about yourself," Tess added. She stiffened. She still experienced a sense of anxiety when she shared in front of the group, but it faded as she was met with reassuring nods from the room.

"Exactly, Tess. And identifying the hesitation is a big first step."

"But what if you don't want to talk about trauma?" Tess darted her gaze in surprise. Her roommate had asked the question.

"That's a hard one," the tech admitted. "It's important to note that you don't have to talk about everything immediately. That doesn't mean you shouldn't go to therapy. Just move at a comfortable pace. Its purpose is to support you, not to trigger you."

Her roommate gave a slow nod, and Tess found herself nodding too.

The group dove into support systems, the idea of letting your friends and family in and allowing them to hold you accountable, and radical acceptance. Accepting their diagnosis. In their position, wishing their life was different wouldn't get them very far.

Eventually, the group dissolved, and another tech rolled in a cart with labeled trays stacked on top. One by one, he called out names and handed out Styrofoam-packed meals. Tess grabbed hers and sat at one of the tables next to Summer.

"Is your boyfriend coming today?" Summer asked, then she stabbed a fork into her pot pie and stuck it in her mouth.

Tess opened her own tray and looked at the food skeptically. She had been wrong to fear the staff. The true horror was the food. "He's not my boyfriend. But yes. He comes every day."

"The funniest thing was when you refused to see him the first couple of times. Poor guy."

Tess grinned at the memory. It wasn't really funny in the moment, but it felt ridiculous now. She had still thought she was making him sick.

"He saw me at my worst, yet he doesn't treat me any differently. I thought if he knew I have bipolar disorder, it would change things between us somehow...and then I thought I wasn't actually bipolar." Tess opened the pack of mandarin oranges that came with her lunch.

"And now?" Summer asked.

"Well, now I'd say it's pretty much confirmed. And also— fuck manic episodes and ever doing that shit again."

Summer laughed. "So, you're gonna take the meds, despite the *flattening*?" She said the last word like a mysterious curse and shook her hands in the air.

"I really harped on that, didn't I?" Tess replied flatly.

"We all heard you arguing with the doctors about it. You guys went back and forth like you were negotiating a war treaty. It seems like it worked out in the end, though." Summer pressed open a milk carton and took a swig.

"Yeah, I feel like myself again. Without the delusions and plus the trauma."

"Second the trauma," Summer muttered, frowning as she glanced down at her food. Her expression shifted back to a smile as she grabbed a couple of orange slices. "You talk to EBN or whatever it was?"

"Yes. I'm out of the contract, but I can't compete or stream for a year—at least on a professional level. It seems like there's a plus side to medical emergencies." Tess had finished her oranges and decided to try the pot pie. For some reason, it tasted fishy."What are you going to do in the meantime?"

"I'll still play for fun, but I'm going to focus more on recovering my mental health this time. I'm going to talk about my experiences with mania, even if it brings up memories that aren't comfortable. I'll start building lifestyle habits that make it manageable. I'm focusing on that until I can focus on the future."

"You sound like a Bipolar PSA," teased Summer.

"Don't mock my progress." Tess grinned.

"I'm sorry, you're right." Her smile stayed playful, but she spoke softly.

Tess opted not to finish the pot pie and dumped the rest of her tray in the trash. She made her way back to her room and resumed reading. The same tech poked her head in an hour later through the door.

"Tess, you have a visitor."

Cade had already made himself comfortable in the visitation room, a frequent guest at this point. He stood up to hug her, and then Tess sat next to him.

"I'm officially out of the contract with EFN," she announced.

His face lit up. "So, we can duo again."

"We can, but no real tournaments for a year." She avoided his gaze, glancing around the room instead.

"Time for us both to get better. You making me extra sick and all," he teased.

She shoved him lightly, and he laughed, fending off her hands. He caught them with his own and held on to them for a moment. The tech overseeing visitation gave them a look and he dropped them again.

"Still blushy," Cade said with a grin.

"Stil egotistical," Tess muttered, but she was smiling as well.

He changed the subject. Partially, she thought, because he refused to admit that he was egotistical. "What did you talk about in your group today?"

"Basically, we talked about what we will do when we get out: go to therapy, accept the diagnosis, and have a support system."

"You know, we're likely to get back to playing every day," Cade said. His tone was often softer when he felt vulnerable. "We could be supports for each other. Check-in and all that. You with your therapy and medication, me with being sober."

"I like that idea," Tess said warmly. She glanced at the phone attached to the hospital wall. "And there's also Andrea for my support system. She calls every day." Tess thought about how Andrea had to contact Cade to tell him about the mania. She felt guilty for never warning him, though she never expected something like this to happen. "I'm sorry I didn't warn you about my mental health. I just didn't tell you because...well, like you said, it was nice having someone who didn't know. Who saw me differently."

"I completely understand, Tess," Cade said. He looked at a painting on the wall and shook his head. "I still feel horrible about where that same idea got me."

Tess leaned in toward Cade. "I know I was pretty out of it when I came and talked to you at first, but I really do forgive you. I understand why you didn't tell me."

He smiled slowly. "I still see you as the same Tess that can take my ass down in a build fight."

She smirked and poked his chest. "It's best you don't forget. I'll be back to competing soon enough. Once the contract duration is up...then what do you want to do?"

He looked smug, "Well, Tess...then we make bank."

She laughed, but the money wasn't really what had her smiling. No, it wasn't the money at all.

Epilogue

The sound of the ocean competed with the murmur of chattering customers at the beachside cafe where Tess was wrapping up her afternoon shift. She slid a customer's credit card through a worn machine, her gaze drifting out the window toward crashing waves.

A tug on her pony-tailed hair pulled her back, and she turned suddenly. Summer stood behind her, grinning with a twenty-dollar bill in her hand.

"One of your tables left this behind. I didn't want to leave it sitting there, waiting to be snatched up."

"So instead, you snatched it up?" Tess asked.

"Essentially," Summer replied with a laugh.

Summer had worked at this cafe for years, and when Tess moved to California, she'd pulled some strings to get her a job there as well. With her winnings from the Grand Championship, Tess didn't need the job, but it felt nice to have a productive way to pass the time before she could compete again. Her mood was easier to manage with a structured routine and a sense of purpose.

Tess stuffed the bill into her apron, then crossed the dining area to drop off a final check. She weaved back through the trendy beach interior to the coffee bar, where Summer already had two iced lattes waiting.

"Mocha for you and caramel for your boyfriend," she said, sliding them forward.

"Thank you," Tess said, smiling at how well her friend knew her and by extension Cade. She fit the lattes into a cardboard carrier. "I hope it doesn't get too crazy for you."

"Bring it on," Summer replied. "All the more tips."

Tess laughed and glanced back to the table where she had dropped off the check. The customers were gone. She collected their signed check and finished her paperwork. On her way out, Summer gave her a quick nod, already preoccupied with more customers.

Outside, Tess breathed in the warm, salty air that was starting to become more familiar. It had been seven months since her hospitalization in California—six months since she'd made the decision to move.

She'd connected deeply with the inpatient program here and wanted to continue her outpatient care with the same team. She found a studio apartment just a few blocks from the cafe and also a few blocks from Cade, which may or may not have influenced her decision.

After completing both inpatient and outpatient rehab, Cade had the charges from the tournament incident dropped. He still attended NA meetings, even though it wasn't required, and it seemed like he truly understood how dangerous his drug use had been.

When Tess first broke the news about moving, her parents were not exactly thrilled. But after a few months, they agreed it was the right decision. She was in a better headspace, and it was hard to deny that moving was a part of that.

Tess walked past her own apartment building and headed for Cade's instead. At his front door, she knocked gently and then pushed it open. An intoxicating teriyaki scent hit her immediately. She looked to the back of the room, where Cade hovered over the stove.

Something she'd learned in counseling was how much nutrition impacted her mood. Ever since she'd mentioned it to Cade, he'd gone crazy researching healthy recipes. Cooking was something he really leaned into after becoming sober. A hobby to keep his hands and head preoccupied outside of gaming.

"Something smells amazing," Tess said. She set the lattes on the counter and peered over Cade's shoulder. He stirred chicken, broccoli, and rice through a thick brown sauce.

"Some say that I'm the best chef in La Jolla," Cade said as he turned to greet her.

Tess rolled her eyes. He leaned in and kissed her. The feeling never lost its magic.

"How was your shift?"

"Not bad," Tess replied. "But I'm eager for the end of my streaming ban."

Cade and Tess both planned to contact Esports teams after that. They planned on only accepting a deal where they could continue to play together. Cade was getting by with an independent stream and tournaments, but Tess couldn't play with him while he was streaming or competing for money.

"It's only a matter of time," Cade said, returning to the stir-fry. "I played some matches with your brother earlier."

"How was that?" Tess asked. It meant so much to her that he made time for him. Tess played with her brother often as well, it was a good way to stay in touch.

"The kid's a fast learner," he replied. "He might be coming for your family title."

"Impossible," Tess joked.

She walked across the kitchen and opened a cabinet, pulling out two plates. Cade turned down the burner and slid the pan across the stove, off the heat. They ate together, discussing their plans for the week and the upcoming DuskCabins tournaments Cade was preparing for. Afterward, Tess collected their dishes and rinsed them in the sink.

In the living room, Cade turned on his Xbox. They were playing through a co-op puzzle game. It was good for days when they wanted to play something other than DuskCabins. Lo-fi loading screen music filled the room as Tess finished scrubbing their plates.

There was a time after her first manic episode when Tess believed life would never return to normal. And then, after her second episode, a period where she thought her life could never be stable. But now, seven months later—with consistent medication, regular sleep, and therapy—her life had stabilized.

Her mood still wavered over long periods, but not in a way that was so extreme that she couldn't maintain her job and relationships. She no longer lost touch with reality the way she did when she was unmedicated.

Maybe her life wasn't 'normal' in the exact same way it had been before her first manic episode. She was on the other side of the country, in love with a man she would have never met otherwise and making a living in the most unexpected way.

But she would take this new normal over the old any day.

Tess spent so long regretting the series of events that led to her hospitalizations—even if she didn't have complete control over it. But standing here now, she didn't regret where she'd ended up. And there was no denying those episodes were part of the road that brought her here.

About the Story

I began this story in college while learning to cope with bipolar disorder myself. Writing about Tess was a very cathartic outlet for me. It helped me process my own experiences. I had fun involving video games as it served as an escape for me, just as it did for Tess.

I was in the creative writing club at my college, and after a long-form critique session, I was encouraged to finish this story. I wrote most of the book while quarantined for COVID, and it sat untouched in my Google Drive folder for a long time after.

A couple of manic episodes later, I transferred to an online college and worked full-time as a waitress. I finally had the money to invest in getting the story out on paper. But, between work and school, I was not able to give the book the attention or edits I had hoped to. I was unhappy with the end product, didn't try to market it, and decided to stop writing.

Four years later, I found my way back to writing again. Now, having earned my bachelor's degree, I have reclaimed my free time outside work. I've started to get involved in writing communities through TikTok, the Orlando County Library System, Discord, and Instagram. I was encouraged not to give up on this story. I decided to pull the original version, make the edits I've always wanted, and publish a version I could be proud of.

There are so many people to thank for supporting me through the first version and the second. My original beta readers: Lauren Judkins, Aabha Vora, Joe Shanley, Carin Colebaugh, Becca Inzer, Brian Liu, Miles Turrell, and Sue Ayres. My new editor: Mallory Day (@mallorydayediting). My new cover designer: Bia S. (@biashuja.designs). My new beta readers: Lauren Judkins, Lauren Ayres, Clark Guire, and W. J. Aaron.

Thanks to every person in every writing group who has inspired me to keep pursuing my dreams. To keep up with my future projects and writing journey join me on Tiktok/Instagram @Kelly.Waters.Auth or visit my website kellychyllenewrites.com. To find all my socials visit: linktr.ee/kellychyllenewaters.